P9-CFO-953

AFTER THE
BUGLES

Forge Books by Elmer Kelton

NOVELS
Barbed Wire
Bitter Trail
Buffalo Wagons
Captain's Rangers
Cloudy in the West
The Day the Cowboys Quit
Eyes of the Hawk
The Good Old Boys
Hanging Judge
Hot Iron
Joe Pepper
Llano River
Many a River
Pecos Crossing
The Pumpkin Rollers
Sandhills Boy
Shadow of a Star
Shotgun
Stand Proud
Texas Rifles
The Time It Never Rained

SONS OF TEXAS TRILOGY
Sons of Texas
The Raiders: Sons of Texas
The Rebels: Sons of Texas

THE BUCKALEW FAMILY SERIES
After the Bugles
Bowie's Mine
Long Way to Texas
Massacre at Goliad

THE TEXAS RANGERS SERIES
Badger Boy
The Buckskin Line
Hard Trail to Follow
Jericho's Road
Lone Star Rising
Ranger's Trail
Texas Vendetta
The Way of the Coyote

THE HEWEY CALLOWAY SERIES
Six Bits a Day
The Smiling Country

OMNIBUS
Brush Country
   (comprising *Barbed Wire* and *Llano River*)

Lone Star Rising
   (comprising *The Buckskin Line, Badger Boy,* and *The Way of the Coyote*)

Ranger's Law
   (comprising *Ranger's Trail, Texas Vendetta,* and *Jericho's Road*)

Texas Showdown
   (comprising *Pecos Crossing* and *Shotgun*)

Texas Sunrise
   (comprising *Massacre at Goliad* and *After the Bugles*)

ELMER KELTON

AFTER THE BUGLES

FORGE®

A TOM DOHERTY ASSOCIATES BOOK
NEW YORK

This is a work of fiction. All the characters and events portrayed in this book are either products of the author's imagination or are used fictitiously.

AFTER THE BUGLES

First published by Ballantine Books in 1967.

A Forge Book
Published by Tom Doherty Associates, LLC
175 Fifth Avenue
New York, NY 10010

www.tor-forge.com

Forge® is a registered trademark of Tom Doherty Associates, LLC.

ISBN 978-0-7653-4302-4

First Forge Edition: June 2004

Printed in the United States of America

0 9 8 7 6 5 4 3 2

AFTER THE
BUGLES

I

THE BODIES WOULD LIE THERE TILL THEY WENT to dust, for Santa Anna had lost the battle. And with the battle, he had lost the war.

His saber-cut arm resting in a loose sling, Joshua Buckalew silently waited while his horse was being saddled. His sober gaze drifted across the still and somber San Jacinto battlefield, where score upon score of lifeless Mexican soldiers lay crumpled on the ground or bogged in black mud or floating in the reedy marshes of Buffalo Bayou. Two days ago a swaggering Santa Anna had gone into his tent for siesta, confident that he held victory in his hands, for he had a ragged rabble of hungry Texans backed against the bayou. He awakened in panic to find the sodden plain slashed by musket and rifle and cannonfire, his red flag trampled by desperate men whose voices clamored in fury above the thunder of the guns: "Remember the Alamo! Remember Goliad!"

Now it was over. The war was won. A victorious army had repaired to its camp at the edge of the plain, shouting for the blood of the captured Napoleon of the West. Big Sam Houston, nursing a shattered ankle, grimly refused to let them have him. Dead men write no treaties, he declared. And Texas would have her treaty of independence.

Home. The exultation had faded now in the barren stillness of the battlefield, and the Texans thought of home. A bitter taste lay sharp in Joshua Buckalew's mouth, for he knew his home lay in ashes. What the retreating Texans hadn't burned, the Mexican army had. He gazed westward, his mind reaching far beyond what his pain-pinched eyes could see. He knew the desolation that waited there: the gutted homes, the burned-out towns, the unmarked graves scattered from here to the Rio Bravo. The land itself still lay there, neglected but otherwise unchanged by the war, still possessed of the elusive promise that had drawn Americans by the thousands into Mexican-owned Texas to colonize under the laws of Mexico. Yes, the land remained, but everything else would have to be built back again with sweat and blood and determination. After all those hard years of work and privation and gradual accomplishment—years that had drifted away in smoke—Joshua Buckalew wondered if he still had it in him.

Times, winning the war is only the beginning of the battle. After the bugles fall silent, there is always the long road back.

Short, shaggy-haired Muley Dodd finished saddling Buckalew's horse and looked worriedly at the sling. "Josh, you reckon maybe we ain't rushin' a mite? You'd travel better if that arm wasn't so angry-lookin'."

Joshua Buckalew had been standing hunched in unconscious deference to the throbbing arm. Now he drew himself to his full five-feet-eleven. "It'll heal as good on horseback as here in this cursed swamp. I've seen enough of San Jacinto to last me a lifetime."

There was another reason to be moving on. He looked gravely at Ramón Hernandez, who finished lashing a blanket-wrapped bundle across the back of a captured

Mexican packhorse. Beneath that blanket lay the body of
Antonio Hernandez. "Ramón wants to bury his brother at
home. If the weather turns warm, we got no time to waste."

In the early 1830's, Joshua Buckalew and his older brother
Thomas had come to Texas from Tennessee to try to build
a home in Stephen F. Austin's new land. They had drifted
west and west and west, until at last they found what they
wanted far beyond San Felipe de Austin, beyond even the
Colorado River, near the Mexican colony where the Hernandez family squeezed a living out of the raw frontier by
plowing their fields and raising cattle and catching wild
horses. The Buckalews, copying the pattern, farmed some
and branded wild cattle and broke mustangs to trade for
supplies and now and again a handful of hard money in the
eastern settlements. It had been a primitive life, in the
main. But the Buckalews by their nature had been west-
moving men, ever since Grandpa had frozen his feet that
winter with George Washington.

Then had come Santa Anna, bringing cannon and sword
to impose a terrible will upon his own people, finally crossing the Rio Grande to lay the same lash across the shoulders of the *Americano* colonists. He had slaughtered his
way up by the Alamo and La Bahia. At Goliad, Thomas
had fallen, cut down with more than three hundred other
helpless prisoners in the shadow of that grim stone
fortress. Joshua Buckalew had been among the fortunate
few who escaped in the confusion of smoke and fire and
dying men.

Now, suddenly, he still didn't completely comprehend
it—the war was over. From Houston's camp the prisoner
presidente had sent orders by courier for all Mexican
troops to retreat beyond the Rio Grande. Texas no longer
belonged to Mexico; it was a free and sovereign republic,

rich in land and hope, but in all other things as poor as Job's turkey.

This was April. Time to go home now and plow the corn.

Muley Dodd pointed westward across the intermittent stretches of water which dotted the greening plain. Heavy rains all month had made eastern Texas a hell for both armies—Mexican and Texan. It would be slow, traveling home. "It's awful far, Josh," Muley worried. "You reckon we can make it there with Antonio?"

Josh shook his head, for he had his doubts. "We'll try."

Except for a bit of sugar, coffee and cornmeal scrounged from among the defeated Mexicans—who were poorly fed themselves—they would have to live off the land. But Texas had deer and wild turkey aplenty, and sometimes bear. Farther west, where the settlements thinned, there would be wild cattle descended from the original mission herds. The diet was monotonous sometimes, but nobody ever starved.

Josh swung carefully up onto his horse, favoring the wounded arm, sucking a sharp breath between his teeth as the pain gripped hard.

Ramón Hernandez' brow creased. "Josh," he said in Spanish, "that arm will give you trouble. Perhaps it is better if you wait a few more days. I can get home alone."

Josh doubted that. A lone Mexican rider caught by a roving Texan patrol would probably be shot before he could bring out his army papers and explain that he had fought in Juan Seguin's Mexican company on the side of Sam Houston. The dark brown man's skin would be taken as evidence enough that he belonged to the enemy.

Josh replied in English. They did that most of the time, the two, each talking in the language that came easiest but understanding the other nevertheless. "I'll heal." He glanced at little Muley Dodd, who was off saying his goodbyes to men he had met in Houston's camp. "Besides, I'll be obliged for your help. Muley's intentions are good, but sometimes his results are poor."

"He fought well," Ramón pointed out.

Josh nodded but held his opinion. Muley had always been what people charitably called "slow." Like some lonesome hound dog, he had attached himself to Josh and Thomas and had trailed along with them all the way down from Tennessee. He had no home, so the Buckalews gave him one. Muley was good help if someone told him what to do; he would break his back without a whimper. But he had to be watched like a child whose curiosity outweighs its judgment.

The matter settled, they rode in silence among the huge old oaks, from which the long beards of Spanish moss hung in cheerless disarray like funeral wreaths. Josh never looked back. Most of the time he gazed through the rain at the trail ahead, though now and again he quietly studied the faces of Muley Dodd and Ramón Hernandez.

Ramón. Pity, what the war had done to Ramón. He had always been the jovial one, quick to smile, quick to sing, the best at roping wild cattle, the quickest to throw a rawtreed Mexican saddle on an unbroken mustang and swing up shouting. His brother Antonio had been the grim one, never smiling, never seeing anything but the flat and the gray and the black. Now Antonio lay wrapped in that blanket, dead, and Ramón had taken on the face of Antonio . . . solemn, unsmiling. It was not a face that fit him. But that was the way of war.

They rode hunched against the slow, chilling rain, minds running over the violence they had put behind them. Ramón's and Josh's, anyway. Muley seldom thought back. His mind was always foraging ahead, flushing out one wild notion after another, the way a pup flushes rabbits but seldom catches one.

Muley's stubbled face twisted as he tried to puzzle

through an idea. "Josh, them fellers at camp, they was tellin' me Texas don't belong to Mexico no more. They was tellin' me it's a republic. That's really somethin', ain't it?"

"I reckon so, Muley."

"I thought it must be." He frowned. "Josh, what *is* a republic?"

"Well, Muley, it's . . ." Josh didn't know quite what to tell him. "It means we're free, Muley. We're independent."

"You mean we're like a slave that's had his chains took off?"

"Somethin' like that. We belonged to Mexico and had to do what they told us to. Now we do what we want to."

"Like, we don't have to work no more unless it suits us?"

Josh scratched his head. "Look, Muley, a man is free, but still he *ain't* free. I mean, nobody can tell him he's got to work, but if he don't, he goes hungry. It's like that with a republic. It's free from other countries, but it ain't ever free from responsibility. It's got to raise food or starve. It's got to make its clothes or go naked. It's got to keep up an army or its enemies will run over it. In other words, it's got to take care of itself. Nobody else is goin' to."

Muley fretted. "Used to, we could just let Mexico worry about all them things. Maybe we was better off when we wasn't free."

Josh shook his head. Trying to explain politics to Muley was like trying to empty a river with a wooden bucket.

Ramón rode along listening, his black-whiskered face furrowed in thought. "His talk is not all foolish, Josh. It is not easy to be free."

"You wishin' we hadn't fought?"

"I wish we had not had to. We fought because of Santa Anna, not because of Mexico herself. It is as if we had to spit in the face of our mother."

"A mother who beat and chastised us?"

Ramón's face was sad. "But still a mother."

Josh knew no way to reply, and he didn't try to. He knew Ramón's tie to Mexico was one of tradition and blood. Josh had felt a strong tie once, too, but mostly one of gratitude for opportunities offered. That tie had not been strong enough to endure, once the trouble began. Josh thought he could understand Ramón's feelings, even though he was unable to share them. And therein lay one of the main factors that had brought difficulty in the first place. The cultural difference between the new *Americano* settlers and the native Mexicans had been too great for deep understanding. Even when the hand of friendship was extended, there had been reservations and mistrust. The settlers tried hard, many of them, but even between good friends such as Ramón Hernandez and Joshua Buckalew there remained that last tiny distance they could never quite reach across, that final measure of understanding that never quite came.

It's not our fault, and it's not theirs, Josh thought. *The Bible said all men would be imperfect. Take a horse to a strange country and he'll always try to go back home, to stay with what's familiar to him. Men are no different.*

They made a long ride in the rain and at dusk camped in the ruins of a homestead the Mexicans had put to the torch. Under a caved-in shed they found blackened wood which hadn't been altogether burned away and which was still dry enough to set ablaze. They made coffee and ate cold *tortillas* and huddled around the meager warmth of the little fire, trying to dry out. The damp cold brought a new ache to Josh's arm, and it showed in his face.

"Josh," Muley worried, "you ain't fixin' to get sick on us, are you?"

"Long as we keep travelin' west, I'll make it."

"Don't you worry none, Josh. I'll take care of you."

The thought was pleasant, if not reassuring.

The rain stopped next morning, but they rode across a trackless country, for any sign of recent movement had been washed away. So far as they could tell, they were the first to travel here since the fighting had ended. They came upon mute evidence of the terrible "Runaway Scrape" which had swept across Texas after the fall of the Alamo and the horror of Goliad. They saw burned-out houses. Along the trail they found abandoned sleds and scattered remnants of the loads they had carried. These had been left behind when the livestock broke down and were unable to pull further, or when pressure of the Mexican army forced fleeing settlers to leave their possessions, mount their animals and make a wild run for the Sabine River and the sanctuary which awaited on the other side.

Twice they came across broken-down wagons, only a fractured wheel and the wagon bed itself remaining, the good wheels having been salvaged. Always they searched the relics for food or useful items, but inevitably someone else had done it first. Whatever one man threw away or abandoned, some other man had need of. Texas had nothing to waste, those days. Nothing but land.

Riding, Joshua Buckalew looked back occasionally in cold regret at the burden which trailed behind on the pack-horse.

The day was long. His arm throbbed with fever, and each step the horse took came as a jolt of pain. The cold *tortillas* lay like lead in Josh's stomach. Muley frowned. "Josh, you ain't lookin' good."

Ramón reined up and pointed his chin. "*Mira, hombre,* over there. I see a trace leading off into that canebrake. It is so faint I almost missed it. If we follow it, we might find something."

After all the years of exposure, Muley had picked up only a smattering of Spanish. He understood only enough to scare him. "Like what?" he asked, full of doubt.

"Whatever it is, it will be no worse than what we have.

Maybe a house the Mexican soldiers missed. Maybe hot food."

"And maybe Mexicans," Muley worried.

Josh had to blink to keep the haze cleared away, for his fever was rising. The trace could have been an old one, not used in a long time. At any rate, it had not been used since the rains. The horses were making tracks six inches deep in the mud. Anyone else's would have done the same. "Let's try it. If we don't find nothin', we can always come back."

The trail meandered through the dense growth. It had been used fairly recently, for cane had been hacked away to clear a path. The horses floundered through the swales, and the packhorse almost fell. Ramón desperately fought to keep it from crushing the body of his brother.

Josh had a futile thought: *It's too far. We'll never get Antonio home.* But he knew that so long as Ramón wanted to, they would keep trying.

They came at length to a sappy-green clearing. A log cabin stood in the center of it. A pair of muddy dogs bounded out to meet them, barking, but they were not hostile. They were tickled to death to see a human being, for they circled around and around the riders and tried to move right under the horses' feet.

"*Hyaww,*" Muley shouted at them, waving his arms. "*Hyaww!*"

The horses snorted and shied. Muley's let fly with a hind foot, narrowly missing the younger and less observant of the dogs. In the yard, hogs grunted and scattered, a pair of them bumping and squealing, teeth flashing. Chickens flapped their wings and fluttered out of the way, clucking and cackling.

Muley grinned, for chickens meant eggs, unless these two dogs abandoned to hunger had been sucking them all. "I could eat half a dozen of them hens, feathers and all."

Ramón said quietly, "This place belongs to somebody."

Muley replied, "He must've lit out in a right smart of a hurry. Probably figured old Santa Anna was grabbin' at his shirttail, him leavin' all this behind."

"He probably intended to come back to it. If we eat his chickens, he will have no eggs. And if he has no eggs, he will have no more chickens."

Seeing disappointment in Muley's eyes, Josh said, "Don't fret yourself, Muley. If we don't find somethin' else, we can kill one of them fat barrows. Man don't get any pig crop out of a barrow."

Josh eased down from the saddle, cautiously holding the arm tight against his ribs but feeling the pain anyway. Muley took his reins. "Go set, Josh. I'll take care of the horse."

The dogs reared up, licking at Josh's hands. One bumped his arm and caused him to double over from the shock of it. Muley came shouting. "Git, dogs! Git, I say!" The dogs took after Muley then. Seemed natural, somehow. Dogs had always taken a liking to Muley, the way they would to a kid. Perhaps they sensed that in ways he was just a boy.

Rain had caused the rough wooden door to swell tight, but Ramón pushed it open. The cabin smelled musty from the rain, and from the fact that all the shutters had been closed. In those times there probably were not three sheets of glass in a hundred miles. Ramón opened the shutters to let the air circulate and told Josh to sit down. But Josh had been in the saddle all day. He wanted to move a little. The arm would hurt anyway.

Muley poked around and discovered a cribful of corn, part of which he shelled for the horses. He brought some to the cabin for supper. Josh found the smokehouse, cured hams hanging from the rafters, and abundant supplies of bacon. Muley took dry wood from under a shed and kindled a blaze in the stone fireplace while Ramón whittled the outer edges off of a ham and threw them to the half-starved dogs. Ramón started coffee boiling in a can and from somewhere rustled up a pan. Muley ground the corn for bread, and they all ate as they hadn't eaten in weeks.

Afterwards, a momentary smile crossed Ramón's face as he leaned back, his stomach full. Josh took pleasure in the sight, for he hadn't seen Ramón smile since San Jacinto. For a while then, Ramón had forgotten the blanket-wrapped burden that lay yonder in the shed, out of reach of the hogs.

Josh said, "What are you thinkin' about, Ramón?"

Ramón's voice was quiet. "Of home. Of Miranda, and the baby I have not yet seen. What do you think of, Josh?"

"Of home. And of a girl."

"María? My sister?"

Josh nodded.

Ramón smiled and changed the subject. "It is a good house, this one."

Josh shrugged. Actually, it was a crude cabin built hurriedly of logs and later chinked with liberal slivers of wood and heavy dabs of plaster in an effort to seal out the wind and rain. But they had been so long out of doors, a chicken coop would look good. "By rights," he said, "they ought to've destroyed this so it wouldn't fall into Mexican hands."

Ramón said, "But aren't you glad they didn't?"

Next morning they ate their fill again. Perhaps it was the food; perhaps it was sleeping dry and warm in a house; but at any rate, Josh felt better. The fever had gone down. He stood in the open door and stared across the clearing into the orange sunrise. Not a cloud was in sight.

Muley said, "I wish we could stay here a week."

Ramón looked gravely toward the shed. "We can't."

"Just wishin', is all."

When the three men rode away, they carried one of the

hams and some bacon from the smokehouse. The rest they left behind, for it belonged to someone else. Maybe he would return, and maybe he wouldn't. In the Runaway Scrape, many hadn't stopped until they had crossed the Sabine River into United States territory. Once there, some would never return to the uncertainties of a land which lay so near to hostile Mexico, no matter how great Sam Houston's victory. But if this one *did* return, he would not find his property looted. At least, not by Josh and Muley and Ramón. They took only what they needed, and in exchange they left behind a Mexican rifle Muley had picked up on the battlefield. A rifle was something a man could always use.

The dogs followed a long way before they gave up and quit, forlorn as lost children. The three riders did not retrace their steps but instead followed a faint old trace that led southwestward. It hadn't been cleared in a long time and was often slow going. The sun had risen halfway to the meridian before they broke out of the canebrakes and into open prairie.

They hadn't gone two hundred yards when suddenly they wished they had stayed longer at the cabin. Half a dozen horsemen appeared unexpectedly in front of them. Josh had seen enough Mexican cavalry the last few weeks that he recognized these at a glance.

The surprise was as great to the Mexicans. They sat staring, not a hundred yards away. Ramón wheeled his mount and pulled the packhorse after him. "Back to the brakes!"

Whatever worry Josh's arm might have been, he forgot all about it. For a wild instant he could hear the guns of Coleto Creek, and the brutal massacre of Goliad. He spurred like a wild man. The horses tried, but their feet dug deep into the wet ground, and their hoofs left a shower of mud behind them. Shots rattled. Ramón shouted, and his horse

went down, sliding on its side. The packhorse jerked free
and kept running. Ramón crawled away from his horse as it
lay threshing. Josh leaned low to pull Ramón up behind his
saddle but to no avail. Ramón tried to get up but went down
again. Blood spread across the torn leg of his trousers.

Josh shouted, "Muley, you keep a-ridin'!"

But Muley had stopped. And then there was no use in
running, for the Mexican soldiers had closed in around
them, and there was nowhere to go. The rifle under Josh's
leg might just as well have been in Tennessee for all the
good it did. The Mexicans would have put half a dozen
holes through him before he could have drawn it. He
looked into their rifles and slowly raised his good arm.

Muley drew close, his face paling. "What'll we do now,
Josh?"

"Pray some. And do what they tell us to. Climb down
slow, so they won't get nervous and shoot you. We got to
see about Ramón."

The Mexicans grabbed the horses as quickly as Josh and
Muley touched the ground. Josh knelt by Ramón. "How
bad, *compadre*?"

His face pinched in pain, Ramón pointed his chin toward
the officer in charge. "Not good. It will be worse, I think.
We will all get a bullet in the head."

The officer dismounted with the flair of a man in triumph. Of all the riders in the patrol, only he seemed to
carry a pistol. The others carried cumbersome rifles or the
clumsy *escopetas* that had enough recoil to knock a man
out of his saddle. The officer waved the pistol and an-
nounced sharply that all three men were his prisoners.

Josh pointed at Ramón and said in Spanish, "This man is
wounded." The officer seemed to ignore Josh. His eyes
were hostile as he stared down at the bleeding Ramón.
"You are Mexican. Why do you ride with these *Americanos*?" Ramón replied cautiously that they were friends.

"No *Americano* can be friend to Mexicans while there is a war."

"There is no war. Not anymore. Have you not heard?"

The officer showed surprise, but he remained wary. "I have heard nothing."

Ramón gripped his leg, his face twisting as the fire of it began to break through the numbness of the first moments. "The war is over. *El general* Santa Anna has ordered all troops across the Rio Grande."

The officer stared at Josh in puzzlement. "Then we have won. But why are these *Americanos* here?"

Ramón shook his head. "Santa Anna did not win. He lost. There was a big battle at San Jacinto. Houston and the *Tejanos,* they won it."

"You lie!"

"It is the truth, I swear by the Holy Mother."

The officer's hard gaze shifted from one man to another. "Men are sometimes known to lie, even by that which is holy."

Josh said in Spanish, "What he tells you is truth."

The officer's pistol wavered. Josh thought he was likely to fire it at any minute. "No *Americano* is to be believed. And a Mexican who would ride with an *Americano* is even worse. I think I will shoot all of you and end these lies."

One of the Mexicans had ridden out after the packhorse, which had stopped at the edge of the canebrake. Now he came leading the animal. The officer turned to Ramón. "What is tied on the horse?"

"My brother."

The officer's eyes widened. Ramón went on painfully, "My brother died in the battle I told you about. We were trying to get him home to bury him in holy ground with my mother and my father."

The Mexican who had fetched the horse said with face

twisting. "He may be telling the truth, *capitán*. Something is dead beneath that blanket."

"Untie it!"

The Mexicans' horses were shying away, their nostrils keenly aware of the smell of death. A couple of the soldiers eased the bundle to the ground. They unwrapped it gingerly, wanting to get the job over with and move away. Josh didn't look as the blanket was pulled back. He didn't want to see. Ramón turned his head away, too. Muley knew no better than to look, and his face went white.

They would never have gotten home with Antonio.

The officer swore. "That is the uniform of a cavalryman."

Ramón nodded, his face grave. "My brother was in the army of Santa Anna."

Only then did Joshua Buckalew begin to doubt that they were all about to die.

II

THE OFFICER MOTIONED FOR THE TWO SOLDIERS to spread the blanket back over the body. They did so hurriedly and moved away. The officer studied Ramón, his disbelief fading. "You say we lost. How badly?"

"Very badly. Many hundreds were killed."

"And *el presidente*? Did he fight gallantly?"

"He fled in the uniform of a common soldier. The *Tejanos* found him anyway. Sam Houston has him as a prisoner. *El presidente* sent messages by courier for all Mexican army units to retreat from Texas."

"We have been on a long patrol. We have heard nothing."

The soldiers showed it. They were ragged and dirty, and some of them looked sick and emaciated. Their threadbare uniforms showed evidence of being rain-soaked many times and drying on their chilled bodies. Santa Anna had brought most of his troops up from deep in Mexico, ill-fed, ill-clothed, poorly prepared for a climate far colder than they were accustomed to.

The officer said to Ramón, "Your brother was in uniform. You are not."

Ramón shrugged. "There were not enough uniforms for

all who volunteered." It was not in Ramón's nature to tell a deliberate lie, Josh knew. But he *could* tell only that part of the truth which would serve to convey a false idea. Josh held his breath, hoping Ramón could get away with it.

The officer still worried. "You say *el presidente* fled. Did he not first lead the charge against the *Americanos*?"

"He did not charge. He was caught asleep."

The officer nodded bitterly. "That, I believe. He has always been a vain fool, Santa Anna. Mexico will be better off without him."

Listening, Josh was surprised. He had not fully understood that many of the Mexican army officers who gave the tyrant their professed loyalty harbored a carefully hidden contempt. They had little genuine regard for the callous bumbler who fancied himself the new Napoleon but sacrificed his soldiers with no more remorse than if they had been pawns in a chess game.

Ramón said, "He has given Texas away."

The officer swore. "After all the blood that has stained this land?" At length he gave the sad Mexican shrug that signified resignation to fate. "Mexico will be better off without Texas. It is too far from the mother country to be of value. It is a back-breaking land, full of trouble and tears. It is not good enough for Mexicans. Let the accursed *Americanos* have it. It will serve them right."

He ordered his men to bind up Ramón's wound. The job done, one of the men motioned toward Josh and Muley. "What of these? Are we to leave Texas and not get to kill even one more *Americano*?"

The officer frowned. "I am tempted, but they are friends of this man. We shall do them no harm. Let them stay and struggle in this hell they call Texas. That is a punishment worse than death." He turned to Ramón and pointed at the blanket. "You said you were taking him home. How far is that?"

Ramón told him. The officer shook his head. "You have carried him too far already. A soldier should be buried where he falls, with honor. We shall bury him here."

"It is not holy ground."

"When it receives the body of a Mexican soldier, it becomes holy."

Ramón made no more protest, for by now he could see his hope had been in vain. Besides, Ramón would be in no shape to ride now, not for several days.

The ground was soft from the rains. Muley and the Mexicans dug with bayonets and their hands and a bucket that Josh carried for boiling coffee. The hole, when they finished, was far from six feet deep, but it was better than the Mexican soldiers were getting at San Jacinto. It was better than the Texans had gotten at the Alamo and Goliad.

The Mexicans crossed themselves and the officer said a short Latin prayer and they covered the hole. They confiscated the ham and bacon, the coffee and corn. They rode south, leaving the three men at the edge of the canebrake.

Ramón sat on the ground, his bandaged leg stretched forward, face pale. "It is not what I had hoped for. But it is better than if we had left him on that slaughtering ground."

Josh said, "He saved us, Ramón. If they hadn't seen Antonio's uniform, they'd have killed us by now."

"God's plan, Josh. This war came between Antonio and me. For a while we were brothers no more, until we found him dead among the enemy at San Jacinto." Ramón made the same shrug of resignation as the officer. "God's plan. Man sees only what lies behind him. God sees what lies ahead."

The wounded horse lay still now. One of the cavalrymen had cut its throat as an act of mercy. Josh's mouth was still dry with the realization that he and his friends had almost ended the same way, and not through mercy. He told Muley to maneuver Ramón's saddle off of the dead horse and put it on the pack animal. Then, somehow, he and Muley got Ramón astride. They had no provisions left, and a long ride was out of the question for Ramón.

"We'll go back to the cabin," Josh said.

If they had to be stranded, this was a good place for a couple of cripples and a slow-moving Muley Dodd, he thought. Food was plentiful, and if it rained anymore the roof wouldn't leak. The settler who had built the place had done well for himself, considering the times. Nobody bragged much in Texas those days because nobody had much to brag about, except perhaps endurance. But this man had a decently tight cabin. He had a good field, chickens, hogs, some scattered few cattle. And from evidence around the shed Josh was sure there had been a team and a wagon, which the settler no doubt had taken with him on the Scrape. Wagons were exceedingly scarce in pre-revolution Texas. A man who owned a wagon was considered well-to-do. If he owned two wagons, he was rich.

They had had a wagon once, the Buckalews. It had gone up in smoke like almost everything else they owned except the land itself.

Josh's arm healed faster than Ramón's leg, for it had several days' start. Mostly they laid around the cabin sleeping, eating, reading the handful of books they found there. Josh read them, anyway. Ramón could understand spoken English well enough but had to pick his way along slowly with printed words and soon wearied of it. Muley couldn't read at all. Muley spent his time running happily with the dogs, chasing after game but seldom catching any. He hunted bee trees, too, for he always had a knack at that. It didn't worry him that he found none. For Muley the fun was in the chase, not in the catching.

Ramón's leg kept him from pacing the floor, physically.

He paced it anyway, in his mind. Josh could read his thoughts almost as well as he could read the books. Up yonder past the Colorado waited Ramón's wife and a new son. Because the time for her delivery was so near, there had been no question of taking her when he went east to join Juan Seguin's Texas-Mexican company. He had counted on the family's Mexican blood to be protection enough from Santa Anna's troops. Though Santa Anna had been ruthless with his own people south of the Rio Grande, up here he considered his war to be with the *Americanos*. His supply lines were stretched a thousand miles or more, so he needed the cooperation of the Texas Mexican people. In large measure he got it, for he had proclaimed this a racial war, the Mexicans standing shoulder-to-shoulder against the evil blue-eyed *extranjeros* who had come from the other side of the Sabine under a gracious dispensation of the mother country and had then turned against her. But there were those such as the powerful Seguins of Bexar who saw Santa Anna as a blackguard and rallied some of the Mexican people to stand against him. That this made them allies of the *Americanos* could not help but cause them doubt and uneasiness at times. But they rallied just the same.

"We'll get home in due time, Ramón," Josh said.

"There is no due time. I want to be there *now*."

"That baby will wait for you."

"That baby will walk before I ever see him. I want to see them all . . . the baby, Miranda, my sister María . . ."

María . . . Josh went silent then, for he also began thinking of María, a tiny girl with raven hair and dark eyes who laughed and sang. It was a memory to make a man look west, and make him itch to be on the move again.

*   *   *

In a few days Josh's arm was no longer sore. All that remained was a little stiffness. He had read all the books and impatiently watched Ramón cripple around with a crude crutch he had whittled out of a limb, wishing the leg would hurry and heal so they could be on their way. Muley didn't care. He was having a good time with the dogs.

Then one afternoon Muley raced for the cabin, shouting, his face flushed with excitement. One of the dogs ran at his heels. Josh could hear the other one down in the meadow, setting up a racket. Instinctively Josh grabbed up the rifle he had brought from San Jacinto.

"Josh! There's people comin'! I seen them. There's people and horses and mules and some wagons."

"Not soldiers? Not Mexicans?"

Muley vigorously shook his shaggy head. "I seen a couple women."

Ramón pushed up from a chair and reached for the crutch. Josh motioned with his hand. "Stay put. If they're Texans and see you, they're apt to shoot first and ask about you later." He stepped out into the yard with Muley.

Muley eyed Josh's rifle with apprehension. "You reckon they'll come a-fightin', Josh? I already had enough fightin'. I sure don't want no more."

Josh shook his head. "Chances are it's the man who owns this place, come back to claim his own."

"Reckon he'll be mad because we been stayin' here, eatin' his vittles?"

"He'll understand. Anyway, that Mexican rifle we're leavin' will pay for all the vittles we could eat if we stayed a month. We ain't killed none of his layin' hens, or none of his sows. We've left the breedin' stock alone."

Three wagons moved out of a patch of cane and into the open meadow, in good view. Besides the teams, Josh figured there must be a dozen or so extra horses, some running loose, some being ridden by men and boys and one by a little girl. A small boy rode a gray mule.

A man in the lead raised his hand, and the procession stopped. The man touched heels to his horse and rode forward in a slow trot, leaving the others behind him. At the distance, Josh couldn't see their guns, but he had a feeling they bristled on those wagons like cactus. Fifty yards from the cabin the rider slowed to a walk and came in warily.

Muley whispered: "Looky there, Josh. He's got a rifle acrost his lap."

"I see it. Stand easy. Try to grin at him, why don't you?"

He said that to ease Muley's mind, for the violence of the past months had bewildered Muley. He was of a simple nature and had never raised his hand in anger against any man. Muley managed a grin of sorts, but his worried eyes showed it didn't go beyond his teeth.

The rider was tall and gaunt, in ragged homespun. Josh took him to be middle-aged until he came close enough for a look at his face. He was a young man. War and hard times had put years on his shoulders that the calendar didn't account for, Josh reasoned. Well, it had been hell for everybody. Big hands, sun-bleached eyes. Farmer, Josh figured, by the look of him. Most people were, in this country. The call for lawyers and such was none too strong. A man worked with his hands and his back. The rider held his left hand up as a sign his intentions were peaceful, but his right hand still gripped the rifle. Josh got a cold feeling he knew how to use it, and well.

"Howdy," Josh said. "Git down and rest yourself."

The man's eyes touched Muley a moment, then flicked suspiciously back to Josh. "Who be you, mister?"

"My name's Joshua Buckalew. This here is Muley Dodd."

"Names don't mean nothin'. I mean, how come you here? This your place?"

"Nope. Thought maybe it was yours. We was on our way home from San Jacinto."

The eyes narrowed. "How do I know you was at San Jacinto?"

"I just told you."

"If you was there, maybe you can tell me which wing Lamar's cavalry took."

"The right."

"And what horse was General Sam ridin' when the charge started?"

"A big white stallion. I don't know what they called him."

The man relaxed. "They called him Saracen." The hand went easy on the rifle. "I thought we was about the first to come back thisaway. When we seen your tracks dried in the mud, we figured you might be some kind of stragglers or renegades, foragin' around to see what you could steal. You already been here some days, I take it."

"We left pretty soon after the battle. We got this far and ran into a Mexican patrol."

The man's jaw tightened. "A patrol?"

"That was some days ago. I expect it's clear enough now. Of Mexicans, anyway."

"Folks in them wagons, they need a good night's rest. Horses need a feed."

"They can get it here. Mexicans must've missed this place."

"I don't expect they missed many." The rider swung down stiffly, for he had been on horseback a long time. He held out his hand. "My name's Ocie Quitman." His gaze was steady and not unfriendly, but Josh saw pain deep in the pale eyes. There was no happiness in this man.

When Josh shook hands with him, Quitman noticed the stiff arm. "You get that at San Jacinto?"

"Saber cut. About healed now."

Bitterly Quitman said, "We all lost somethin' to Santa
Anna. I wisht they'd of let us hang him. Him and all the
rest of them. I wisht there was dead Mexicans strung on
every tree limb from here to the Rio Grande!" His eyes
hardened, and a cold shudder ran down Josh's back as he
sensed the depth of Quitman's hatred.

*Man, whatever you lost, it must have been really some-
thing.*

Quitman waved, and the wagons moved again, the lead
wagon's canvas sagging on uneven hoops that seemed to
shift with each jolt of the wheels on the rough ground.
Towering in the seat, hunched over the leather lines, was a
big, square-shouldered, middle-aged farmer. His raw-
boned wife sat beside him, her face all but hidden beneath
a sagging bonnet. Halting his team, the big farmer handed
the reins to the woman and climbed down, walking toward
Josh, extending a huge hand that looked as if it could smite
a mule to its knees. "Howdy, friend. We're sure glad to see
a new face after all these days. My name's Aaron Provost.
This here your place?"

Josh told him it wasn't, that they had stopped here to re-
cuperate.

Provost said, "We was a little concerned at first over who
you might be, but you got a good face."

Josh felt his bewhiskered cheek and wondered how the
farmer could tell. He couldn't remember when he had
shaved. "You got a lot of people here."

"That yonder's my wife Rebecca. Them young'uns you
hear whoopin' and hollerin' back there with the stock . . .
the missus and I are responsible for all of them but one.
The Lord's been more bountiful with children than He has
with some of the other blessin's." He didn't say it as if he
were complaining, and Josh doubted that Provost regretted
sowing the seed. Provost pointed a thick finger. "Fellers on
that middle wagon, they're Wiley McAfee and his partner

Dent Sessum. That last wagon yonder, it belongs to Ocie Quitman."

Josh saw a woman sitting on the seat, handling the lines. "I suppose that's Mrs. Quitman."

Ocie Quitman turned away. Provost said, "No, it's the Widow Winslow. Heather Winslow. Husband fell to the Mexicans a while back. Ocie let her have the borrow of his wagon. That lad on the gray mule, he belongs to Ocie."

"How far you-all goin'?"

"Long ways yet. Rebecca and me, we had us a place up on the Colorado. The Quitmans, the Winslows, they was all nearby. Sessum and McAfee, they got no land as yet. They're just lookin'."

Josh counted the men who could use guns. "You got four men who can shoot if it comes necessary."

"Five. My eldest, Daniel, ain't but fourteen, but he's a right peart shot when he has to be."

"He might have to be. Last I knew, Comanches was prowlin' the western country, lookin' for easy pickin's. Didn't take them long to find out about the war. Them slow wagons make a good target of you."

Ocie Quitman came back. "Whichaway was *you* headed, Buckalew?"

"West."

"If you was to join up with us, that'd be seven guns."

"Eight. We got one more man in the cabin. Mexican patrol put a bullet in his leg."

Two dusty, lanky men in homespun and buckskins shared a whisky jug, then climbed down from the second wagon and lazily stretched themselves, one of them scratching his ribs. They didn't offer the jug to anyone else. One chunked a rock at the barking dogs. The other hungrily eyed the chickens. Josh featured them as being likely to spend a lot more time in the woods than in the fields.

The woman on the third wagon had her face shaded by a

large bonnet similar to Mrs. Provost's, but when she turned toward Josh, he caught a glimpse of her features. He judged she was in her mid-twenties. The little boy reined his gray mule up beside her and stuck close, his large brown eyes abrim with curiosity as he stared at Josh and Muley, and with joy as he looked at the dogs.

Josh said, "She don't look old enough for a widow."

Provost replied, "Wartime, it don't take long."

"She's got no business goin' west again, a woman by herself."

"It's her land, and she's got no place else to go. No people left back in the States."

"She can't work a farm."

"She's stronger than she appears to be. Give her a few years and she'll look like my Rebecca yonder." Josh couldn't see that as a recommendation, but the farmer seemed to think it was. "Anyway, she's got determination. That counts for as much as muscle. And she's a fair handsome woman. I expect there'll be bachelors enough more than willin' to lend a hand." Provost appraised Josh with a wry squint. "You a bachelor, Buckalew?"

The dogs quit barking when the kids started hitting the ground. They made the rounds of first one child, then the next, tails twitching. A smile stretched across Muley's face, for Muley and dogs and kids had always been a happy combination. Before the war, he had gone often to laugh and run with Ramón Hernandez' kid brothers and sisters. Most of them were growing up now, but Muley never would.

Mrs. Provost took charge, shouting orders to the boys and girls from her perch on the wagon seat. The chickens fluttered and cackled in alarm as the youngsters ran around the yard to loosen their tired legs, the dogs yipping merrily after them. The man named Dent Sessum took a few steps in Josh's direction, impatience in his eyes. When Provost strode off to his wagon to speak with his wife, Sessum muttered, "A damned menagerie, that's what it is."

Dryly Ocie Quitman said, "*They* invited *you.*"

Provost tramped back in a few minutes, leading his sun-browned wife by one arm. The young widow followed a few paces behind. "Rebecca . . . Heather . . . this here is Joshua Buckalew. I do believe that if we tried right hard we could talk him and his party into throwin' in with us as far as Hopeful Valley. We sure could use their company."

Mrs. Provost smiled pleasantly and proceeded to look Josh up and down as if she were buying a workhorse. She was a weathered but hardy woman who looked as if she could stand up to just about anything chance might decide to throw at her. Most of the early Texas women were that way. Those who weren't either died off or went back to where they had come from. Josh could feature Mrs. Provost skinning game, dressing a baby, quoting Scripture and cussing the weather all at the same time.

Heather Winslow said, "Mister Buckalew may not know me, but I know him."

Surprised, Josh stared. She slipped the bonnet back from her face. "Your farm was west of ours, a good ways. One time you stopped at our cabin on a trip to San Felipe with the old surveyor, Jared Pounce. Whatever became of Mister Pounce?"

"He was in the Alamo."

Her mouth went into a thin, sad line. "He was a good man. They were all good men." She dropped her chin and turned away. Josh figured she was thinking of her husband. He vaguely recalled now, though he wouldn't have if she hadn't spoken up. Jared Pounce, always fond of good vittles, had called her the "corn-dodger woman." She was smallish but strong. She had large blue eyes that would catch a man's gaze so that he didn't pay much attention to whether the rest of her was handsome or not. Josh would have considered her pleasant to look upon, though he would have hesitated to call her pretty. *María Hernandez* was pretty.

He said, "I remember. You-all had you a nice place started."

"It could've been a real good place. Lord knows my Jim tried. Seemed like bad luck always dogged him one way and another. Finally came the Scrape, and the Mexicans caught up to us while we were trying to reach the Sabine." She paused. "Do you remember my Jim?"

He shook his head. "Met him once, is all. I'm afraid I wouldn't know him if he was to come ridin' up here."

Sadness lay like blue ice in her eyes. "I wish he would. But he never will, not ever again."

Dent Sessum shouted to his partner, "Wiley, we're goin' to have fresh meat on the table tonight. See that fat sow yonder? She'd feed all of us for a month." Sessum walked toward her, rifle in hand, moving as if to haze her away from the wagons and shoot her.

Josh called to him, "There's cured meat in the smoke-house. You leave the man's livestock alone."

Sessum turned defiantly. "They ain't yours."

Josh moved closer to him. "They ain't *yours,* either. You'll eat cured pork, and you'll leave the sow to fetch more pigs."

For a moment he figured he was fixing to get an argument from Sessum. And if he did, he'd probably have Wiley McAfee to contend with too. Sessum muttered, "Some people act like they was meant to rule the whole blessed earth." But he turned on his heel and walked away from the sow.

Quitman said, "For what it's worth, Buckalew, they ain't no partners of mine."

Josh glanced at Aaron Provost, who seemed to feel obliged to explain his own position. "They had their own wagon, and they had guns. I figured we needed both."

Josh said, "I been hopin' when the war was over, we'd have a lot of new folks come in . . . folks of the better sort."

Quitman said: "These ain't the ones you been waitin' for, then. They was on the Sabine when the fightin' was goin' on at San Jacinto. But the Lord makes all kinds."

The big farmer remarked, "The buzzard as well as the eagle. The sparrow as well as the hawk."

They turned toward the cabin. Provost said, "We best see if the place can be made comfortable for the women-folk. They'll enjoy sleepin' under a roof. God knows they probably won't find one when they get home."

Ramón Hernandez had pushed to his feet. He hobbled to the door, leaning on the crutch.

Heather Winslow's hands went flat against her cheeks, and she screamed.

A hissing sound broke from Ocie Quitman. His rifle swung up. "A Mexican! A damned dirty Mexican!"

Josh grabbed the gun barrel, thrusting it aside. "Hold on! He's with us!"

He had expected momentary hostility; after the last few months it was only natural. But he was not prepared for the fury in Quitman's tight-drawn face. He wrestled with the man, who tried to wrench the rifle free of Josh's grasp. Instinctively Josh knew Quitman would kill Ramón if given the chance. Sharp pain lancing through his stiff arm, Josh shoved the weapon forward, jamming it into Quitman's belly. He jerked it to one side, wresting it from the big hands as Quitman coughed for breath. Quitman kept grabbing for the rifle as Josh stepped back. Josh blew the powder out of the pan.

"Quitman, I told you he's with us. He fought at San Jacinto too."

Quitman struggled for breath. "The hell! Which side was he on?"

"He was with the Juan Seguin company."

Quitman stopped trying then, his fists still clenched, his

face dark. He stared at Ramón with eyes that wanted to kill.

Josh said: "You're not goin' to hurt him. He's my friend."

Quitman stared a moment longer at Ramón, then the sudden rage began to ebb. "To you, maybe, but not to me. No Mexican will ever be a friend of mine again."

He turned and strode toward the wagons, leaving Josh standing there with the rifle in his hand.

III

As Quitman neared Sessum and McAfee, Sessum spoke, "Just say the word, Ocie. We'll kill that Mexican for you."

Quitman made no reply.

Josh dropped Quitman's rifle to the ground and brought up his own, backing toward the cabin door, tensed and ready. The children had stopped running and stood watching open-mouthed. Aaron Provost had turned to watch Quitman, to see what he would do. But Quitman did nothing, except keep walking away. He strode past Sessum and McAfee as if they were not there. He didn't stop until he reached his wagon that the widow had been driving. He leaned against a rear wheel, his back turned, one hand gripping a spoke as he wrestled with whatever private devil was tearing at him.

Mrs. Winslow stood where she had been, except that she had turned away from Ramón, her face paled, still twisted with the shock.

Josh thought now was the time to make one thing clear to everybody. He brought his rifle up across his chest, not pointing it at anybody but letting it be seen. What he had to say would be blunt, but it would not be misunderstood. "Get this down and be damned sure you swallow it, all of you. We're willin' to join you, but we don't have to. We got by before you came, and we can get by if you leave. If you want us, you got to take all three . . . me and Muley *and* Ramón. Anybody that moves a hand against Ramón has got me to whip."

Sessum muttered, "We fought a war to get rid of them Mexicans."

"Way I hear it," Josh spat, "*you* didn't fight nobody."

"We stood guard at the river. Somebody had to. Ain't our fault we never got to kill no Mexicans."

"You're not killin' this one. You better get that through your head."

Aaron Provost frowned, studying Ramón. "How long you known him, Buckalew?"

"Since we first come down from Tennessee."

"And you're sure of him?"

"As sure as I am of myself."

"Well, you're a man who's pretty sure of himself. Me, I didn't worry over Mexicans one way or the other before the war. They went their way and I went mine. Live and let live, was the way I seen it. If you stand up for him, he's all right as far as I'm concerned." Provost turned to face the other men. "We agreed when we started out that if there come a disagreement, we'd take a vote. So we'll decide whether we want Buckalew and his bunch to go with us. Whichever way it comes out, we don't bother Buckalew's Mexican. How about it, you boys?"

Sessum grumbled, "Damn Mexican is apt to stab a man in the back when he ain't lookin'. We ought to shoot him and be safe."

Provost's voice was as big as the man himself, when he became aroused. "But you ain't goin' to, is that understood?" Sessum reluctantly nodded, and McAfee followed suit. It seemed to Josh that whatever Sessum did, the other one tried to do the same. The farmer turned and called after Quitman. "Ocie, how about you?"

Quitman didn't answer until he was asked the second time. Slowly he turned his head. "Just keep him out of my sight!" He walked off beyond the wagon and stood looking across the meadow.

The farmer turned dourly to Josh. "We'll wait awhile to take that vote. Let Ocie have time to get hold of himself and think things through."

Josh said, "I reckon I already know how he'll vote."

"Don't be too quick to put a judgment on him. That'd be as unfair to him as he was to your Mexican. Ocie's got cause to hate. At least, he thinks so. And he's a good man to have on your side. I don't think I'd want him agin me."

Josh had already decided that. But Ramón had a prior call. Right now it didn't look as if there was a place for both of them.

Provost walked away with his wife. Heather Winslow said, "Buckalew . . ."

"Yes?"

"I didn't mean to set things off. It isn't like me to scream. But I didn't expect to see him. He just bobbed up there all of a sudden. He's the first Mexican I've seen since . . ." She looked at the ground.

Josh said, "Don't blame yourself."

She turned and looked toward Ramón, and Josh could tell it was an effort for her. Ramón stood in the doorway. He hadn't moved an inch.

"I'm sorry," she told him.

Ramón said in forced English, "It is for nothing. I did not mean for to scare you, *señora*."

"And I didn't mean to cause you any trouble."

Josh said, "Looks like trouble would've come whether you'd screamed or not."

Mrs. Winslow said, "I want you to know this, Mister Buckalew, if they let the women vote, I'll vote for all of you to go along."

Josh glanced at the wagon where Quitman had disappeared. "What about him?"

"What *about* him?"

"You ridin' on his wagon and all, I thought . . ."

Her blue eyes hardened a little. "Ocie Quitman is a kind man, inside. He saw I needed help, and he gave it. In return, I've been taking care of his little boy. I still think for myself."

"No offense meant, ma'am. I just didn't want to be the cause of trouble between you and him if there *was* anything . . ."

"There is not. Mister Quitman is a gentleman."

"I never thought no other way."

The new arrivals unloaded what they would need out of the wagons and hobbled the teams out on the meadow. When the men had finished the necessary chores, Aaron Provost summoned them all back beside his wagon. He cast one frowning glance at Josh and Ramón, then turned to the others. "Ain't no need us waitin' no longer to take a vote. We'd just as well get the air cleared so this thing don't lie there and simmer between us all night."

Ocie Quitman jerked his head toward Rebecca Provost and Heather Winslow. "How about the women? They get to vote?"

"You got any objection to it, Ocie?"

"Everything we do affects them the same as us. I say give them a vote."

Aaron nodded. "Suits me. Dent . . . Wiley . . . how do you-all feel about takin' Buckalew and his friends?"

Sessum scowled. "The Mexican too?"

Watching silent anger rise in Ramón, Josh said, "It includes him."

Sessum spat on the ground. "Then I say the hell with it." McAfee agreed. "We got on pretty good so far. We can do without them."

Aaron switched his gaze to Quitman. "Ocie?"

Quitman stared at Ramón. "I say no."

Aaron grimaced. "That's three against. Well, I don't agree. I think we're apt to be glad we took them along, even if one of them *is* a Mexican. I don't reckon the good Lord asked him his preference." He glanced at his wife. "Whatever I say, Rebecca will agree to. So I cast our two votes for takin' them with us. Heather, how do you vote?"

Josh was watching Quitman when Heather Winslow half whispered, "They ought to go with us. I vote yes." Surprise flickered in Quitman's eyes, and disappointment.

Aaron said, "Well, that winds us up in a tie. What do we do now?"

The silence hung so hot Josh thought he could light a fuse with it. Finally Quitman shrugged. "If the womenfolk feel better to have them come along, so be it. But keep that Mexican out of my way! I don't even want to look at him!"

Aaron frowned. "Ocie, you have to understand that the war is over. As the Book says, we shall beat our swords into plowshares, and the lion shall lie down with the lamb."

Dryly Quitman replied, "They may lie down together, but the lion will be the only one that gets up."

Ramón moved out of the cabin when the women moved in. Both were silently apologetic. Ramón hobbled out to the shed on his cane while Muley and Josh carried their few belongings. Muley said, "Josh, how come they got it in for old Ramón the way they do?"

"Temper of the times, Muley. Me and you, if we was to go to Mexico we'd get treated the same way."

"It don't hardly seem fair."

"Nothin' is fair in war. Or in what follows after the war, either. Not here, not in Mexico, not noplace."

"Old Provost was right when he said the Lord didn't give Ramón no preference. Reckon if He had, old Ramón would've chosen to be American like us?"

"That's hard to say, Muley."

Muley's face brightened as he examined other angles of the notion. "The Lord didn't give *me* no preference, neither. You know somethin', Josh? If He *had,* I'd of sure been different than I am. I swear, I'd sure ask for a change."

"You would?"

"Yes, sir! I'd have brown eyes instead of blue ones."

They dropped their gear on the packed ground in the rude shed. Ramón carefully lowered himself to a sitting position, stretching his leg out in front of him. His eyes were averted from Josh, but the quiet anger clung to him like heat around a bad stove.

Josh said, "You oughtn't to blame them too much, Ramón."

Ramón gritted in Spanish, "That is what I keep trying to tell myself, but I can't hear it."

"We don't have to go with them. We'd figured all along on goin' by ourselves. We could get up and strike out in the mornin' and on to the Colorado River. We could even leave tonight."

The Provost children and the Quitman boy had followed at a respectful distance. For a few moments they stared from across the open corral that closed off the south side of the shed. Gradually they edged closer, poised to break and run if anybody raised a hand. Their attention was riveted to Ramón, their curiosity gradually overcoming the fear they had for his darker skin. A couple of the children whispered in the little Quitman boy's ear, and he firmly shook his head. They whispered again, nudging him forward. The boy took a few hesitant steps, glancing back over his shoulder to see if his friends were backing him up.

They had been around Mexicans before, Josh reasoned; they *must* have. But Ramón was probably the first they had seen since the Runaway Scrape.

The boy tried to speak but couldn't bring it out. A larger Provost boy stepped up and whispered in his ear again. Finally the little one blurted to Ramón, "Is it true? Are you really Santa Anna?"

Ramón held his silence a moment, his face unreadable. Finally a faint humor gleamed in his black eyes, and for a second Josh thought he was going to smile. "No," Ramón replied in English. "I am not Santa Anna. I am Sam Houston."

The boy's eyes widened in surprise. The other youngsters began to snicker, and the Quitman boy gradually realized he had been taken. "Awwww, you're not."

The other youngsters tittered and ran. The Quitman boy suddenly realized he stood all alone, and he whirled, racing across the corral and scaling the fence.

Ramón watched them go, and the gleam remained. "The wagons are slow. Do you think they will run into trouble?"

Josh said, "You never can tell about Comanches. They could be out west huntin' buffalo, or they could be up this-away huntin' hair to braid their leggin's with. Not likely there's any Mexican soldiers left, but you couldn't take an ironclad oath on that either."

"And *renegados*?"

"Renegades, you got any time you have a war. Sneakin' around the brush pickin' up the leavin's, stealin' what they can, killin' if it comes handy."

Ramón said, "This war is not the children's doing. I have a son of my own now. If harm came to these little ones, and

I had not done what I could, I would not feel entitled to enjoy my own son."

"Folks may treat you dirty, even when you help them."

"I have been treated dirty before. I have not died from it."

Bye and bye Heather Winslow came with a can of steaming coffee and some fried bacon. "Mister Buckalew, Mister Dodd, supper's ready up at the cabin. I brought this out for your friend. With his bad leg and all, I thought he'd rather not have to walk."

She glanced at Josh with apology in her eyes for the weak lie. Ramón accepted the food and coffee with dignity and quiet "*gracias,*" but Josh knew he held no illusions.

Heather Winslow paused, looking back at Ramón with regret. "I am sorry, *señor,* for the way things are. Maybe they won't always be."

Ramón thanked her quietly, then stared at the plate. At length he asked, "Do you think it will get better, Josh?" Then he answered his own question. "No, it will get worse. It may get much worse."

They ate breakfast before daylight. Josh and Muley took theirs to the shed, along with Ramón's. They had decided that if Ramón wasn't welcome in the cabin, they wouldn't go either. After breakfast the men and boys hitched teams to the wagons and brought up the loose stock. Muley and Josh saddled their horses.

Ramón said, "Saddle mine too, will you, Josh?"

"With that leg, you'd better ride in a wagon."

"Which wagon?" Ramón grimaced. "The farmer Provost, he might take me, but his wagon is too loaded. McAfee and Sessum, they would not let me ride on their wagon even if I wanted to. And I do not want to."

"There's still the wagon the widow drives . . ."

"She would say yes, but the wagon belongs to Quitman,

no es verdad? I have no wish to cause her trouble from him. She is a widow. She will have need of him, I think."

"I'll talk to Quitman."

Ramón shook his head. "The leg is not so bad that I cannot ride. I will not beg or owe a debt to anyone. No one can later say he did a big good for this Mexican!"

Rebecca Provost took charge of loading her wagon, shouting orders to the children, who seemed endless in number, the way they swarmed over, around and through the wagon, getting the load settled and tied. Before long the Provost and Winslow wagons were ready to go.

"You-all roll out," Sessum told Provost. "Me and Wiley, we got somethin' to fix. We'll catch up to you directly."

Josh rode by their wagon and failed to see anything that appeared to be broken down. It would have suited him just as well if the two didn't catch up at all. Aaron Provost flipped his lines, shouting roughly, and his team strained against the traces. Heather Winslow followed, shouting in a voice that lacked the coarseness of Rebecca Provost's but which carried authority, nevertheless. Quitman's small son rode the gray mule again, dropping back to join the Provost youngsters in herding the loose stock a short way behind the wagons. The children whooped and frisked along. Whatever terror they had been through, they had shrugged it off. Or at least it appeared they had. Josh wondered, though, if sometimes it would not come back to them in the night, in the screaming horror of a nightmare that the mind is helpless to shut out. War had a way of leaving scars that didn't show.

The dogs followed the youngsters. Aaron yelled back for the kids to chase the dogs home, but nothing worked, not even chunking rocks at them. The dogs would tuck their tails between their legs, drop back a little but continue to follow.

Josh rode up beside the Provost wagon. "Looks like

they're bound and determined to go. They been left here too long to want to stay."

Provost frowned. "I hate to git away with a man's dogs."

"He may not come back. You don't mind your kids havin' the dogs, do you?"

Aaron shook his head. "They ain't likely to have much else when we get home." Rebecca Provost nodded in solemn agreement. "War and hard times has robbed these young'uns. A dog or two would be good for them."

"Then," Josh said, "let's don't worry about it. A hog or a cow is property, but a dog is a free agent. He goes where he wants to and does as he pleases. If it pleases him to tag along with your young'uns, who's to blame?"

Presently, looking back, Josh could see the third wagon moving along, making some progress but showing no hurry about catching up. Every little while he would look back and gauge how much distance it had closed. The rate Sessum and McAfee were traveling, they wouldn't be up to the other two wagons till the noonday stop.

Suspicious, Josh turned his horse and started back toward the trailing wagons. Muley shouted, "Josh, where you goin?"

"You stay here, Muley. I'll be back directly."

He heard a horse loping up behind him and turned to speak sharply to Muley. He saw Ramón instead, the wounded leg thrust out. "Ramón, you just as well stay with the wagons."

"I am curious too."

"It'd tickle them to find an excuse to shoot you."

"I have been shot at by better men."

"You bein' there might cause trouble that I wouldn't otherwise have. I'd rather you stayed here, Ramón."

Reluctantly Ramón reined up. "I will watch from here. If it looks like a fight, I will come."

Josh rode in a slow trot. Approaching the wagon, he

could see hostility. Sessum said, "You needn't have fretted none about us, Buckalew. We're gettin' along just fine."

Josh didn't say so, but that was the thought which made him fret. Tied to the rear of their wagon he saw chicken coops, quickly and crudely put together. He said brittlely, "Looks to me like you're doin' a mite *too* well. I told you yesterday, the breedin' stock belongs to somebody. You got no business takin' it."

"He may never come back."

"On the other hand, he might come back today. Ain't no use you robbin' him."

Sessum argued, "Think how good it'll be, havin' fresh eggs every day we're on the trail."

Josh was sure that even if they *did* have eggs, they wouldn't give him any. He judged the distance back to the cabin and decided the chickens would work their way home if he released them here. "You'll open them coops and dump them chickens out."

Sessum said stiffly, "We hadn't figured on it."

"Then figure on it now. Either you dump them out or *I* will."

Sessum's eyes narrowed. "Just because you done a little soldierin', you don't need to think you can run over the rest of us."

McAfee put in with a sneer, "Anybody who runs around with a stinkin' Mexican has got no call to think he's so much."

Josh rode toward the coops. The two men had packed so many chickens that half the birds would smother before the day was out.

Josh heard a metallic click that brought up the hair on his neck. Sessum gritted, "You touch that coop, Buckalew, and that Mexican is goin' to be awful lonesome, just him and that halfwit."

That was what did it, his calling Muley a halfwit. Josh

reined around, turning his back on the coop. He took a hard
look into Sessum's eyes and decided the man didn't have
the guts to pull that trigger. Josh moved straight at the rifle.
He grabbed the barrel of it with both hands and thrust the
stock back as hard as he could. Caught by surprise, Sessum
took the blow in the belly. He doubled over, coughing for
breath as Josh jerked the rifle out of his slackened hands.
Josh eased the hammer down and pitched the weapon out
into the grass. Turning, he slipped a knife out of its sheath
at his belt and slashed at the nearest coop. It was almost
open when he heard the scuffling of heavy boots. He
looked back to see Sessum climbing across the loaded
wagon.

Sessum leaped at him. The impact and Sessum's weight
dragged Josh out of the saddle and jarred him against the
ground. The horse jerked loose and trotted away. Sessum
pounded Josh with his fists. Josh tried to fend him off with
his stiff arm while he struggled to free the other arm,
pinned beneath him. He gripped Sessum's collar and
yanked, then shifted his own weight and pulled the good
arm out. Wrestling in the grass, the two men rolled into a
narrow ditch that runoff waters had cut across the sloping
hillside. Somehow Josh landed on top of him. He shoved
his knee into Sessum's belly and took most of Sessum's
breath. That put both of them on a fairly even basis, for the
fall from the horse had taken most of Josh's.

Sessum wheezed, "Wiley, come help me."

But the struggle had excited the team, and McAfee's
hands were full with the reins, fighting to keep the horses
from running away. Josh picked up the knife from where it
had fallen and finished slashing the coop open. The chickens rushed out with a flapping of wings and a sudden burst
of squawking. Some landed on Sessum in their first attempt at flight. He threw his arms over his face, cursing.
The horses kept dancing, wanting to run.

Josh started on the second coop as Sessum brushed the chickens away and pushed to his feet, feathers clinging to his dusty clothes. He rushed, cursing. Josh dropped the knife and met him halfway. He gave him a couple of underhanded licks he had learned back in Tennessee. They weren't fair, but no fight is fair unless you win it. Josh had no intention of losing this one.

Sessum doubled over. The horses had quit straining, and McAfee jumped down, ready to join the fight. But he stopped as a dark shadow fell across him. Ocie Quitman sat there on his horse. Behind Quitman, Ramón loped up, his leg outthrust.

Quitman said, "You better hold on, McAfee."

McAfee protested, "He don't look like God to me. He's got no call to be a-tellin' us what to do."

Quitman said calmly, "Then forget what he told you, and listen to what *I* tell you. Turn the rest of them chickens out."

McAfee pointed toward the other two wagons, which had halted. "They're takin' the dogs with them. I don't see where there's no difference in takin' the chickens and takin' the dogs."

"Only way them dogs would stay here would be if you tied them, and then they'd starve to death. But the chickens will stay if you don't tote them off. And you're not goin' to." His eyes were sharp as fine-honed steel. "Now do what I said and open them other coops."

Sessum was on his feet now, glaring at Josh but not putting up any resistance to Quitman. There was a look about Quitman which reminded a man of a loaded rifle, pointed straight at him. Sessum picked up Josh's knife from the ground and cut the coops open, releasing the rest of the chickens. Feathers floated in the morning breeze. Done, Sessum hefted the knife, then hurled it sideways at Josh. Josh's instinct was to duck away from it, and he had to go and fetch it after it fell.

By now Ramón had arrived, but there was nothing for him to do except watch. He did that in silence.

Sessum jerked his chin at Josh and said to Quitman, "I don't know what you have to go and take up his fight for. None of us ever even seen him till yesterday."

"It ain't for him. I just believe in doin' what's right, and carryin' off a man's chickens ain't right. You ought to see that for yourselves."

"All I can see is this Buckalew, makin' out like he was the Lord of all Creation."

"Forget about Buckalew, then. You just worry about *me*."

Quitman turned his horse and started back toward the other wagons. As if he considered the incident over and done with, he never looked behind him.

"That man," Ramón murmured, "is like ice in the river."

Josh said: "I'd sure rather have him for me than against me. Right now I don't think he's either."

Ramón observed, "He is against *me*."

IV

HEATHER WINSLOW LET THE LEATHER LINES sag in her hands as the wagon creaked slowly through the greening grass. Now and again her eyes followed the hopping frogs, brought out by the recent long spell of rains. She flinched each time a wagon wheel crushed one, its body making a distinct "pop" as it exploded under the weight of the iron rim. She was glad Quitman's boy Patrick was back yonder on that gray mule, riding with the Provost youngsters, for it upset him to see the frogs die. He had seen too much of death already for a boy of five.

She glanced back over her shoulder when she sensed that the children had grown quiet for the first time all day. They rode sleepily in the pleasant warmth of the midafternoon sun, loose-herding the extra stock, keeping it drifting along after the wagons. She sought out Patrick and beckoned until he saw her. He rode up, trying to push the lazy mule into a fast trot but unable to get him out of a walk.

"Sleepy, Patrick? Why don't you crawl up here with me and take a nap?"

He nodded. "All right, Mrs. Winslow." She had tried to get him to call her Heather, but the training was too strong in him. A boy called a grown woman Miss or Mrs. That was Ocie Quitman's teaching. She stopped the wagon to let him tie the mule at the tailgate. Climbing up, he stretched his short frame in the wagonseat, legs hanging over the edge, his head in the woman's lap. She flipped the reins and set the team to moving again.

She stared down at Patrick as he drifted into slumber, trying to find in his features those points that resembled his father.

It had always been a disappointment to her that she had never been able to give Jim a son. She didn't know whether the trouble had been with him or with her, and it didn't matter now. At least Quitman had the boy as a tangible reminder of his wife. Heather Winslow had only a memory of Jim, and a piece of land that might have nothing left on it but ashes.

Ahead yonder, a few days up the trail, waited the farm. She had tried to make plans, tried to decide how she could operate it by herself. There would be the fields to work, the garden to tend, the stock to take care of . . . if she had any left. In all probability there would even be a cabin to build. In all the long miles west from the Sabine she had seen only one left intact.

The farm had been hard enough even when Jim was alive. Lord knew he had tried. He'd always had good intentions, Jim had. He had been given to melancholy periods when things didn't go right, but he never complained aloud or blamed anybody. He always tried again. And often as not, he fell short again. Seemed things had a knack of going only halfway for Jim. Never total failure, but never actual success. Heather had tried to rationalize that they expected too much from this raw land, that they should be content with less. But other men did better. Other men worked no harder but came up with better crops. Other men seemed to go farther on good luck than Jim did by breaking his back.

Heather hadn't realized this when she married him. Orphaned young back in Missouri, she had been brought up by her grandmother and grandfather, who were kindly and well-meaning but hard-pressed to raise her after having finished with their own brood and being well along in years. Jim Winslow had come along, a handsome young man full of promise if short of the world's goods. He talked of going to the new land of Texas to seek his fortune and of wanting a nice girl to share it with him. The old folks pushed her to take advantage of the opportunity before some wiser girl beat her to it. She accepted their judgment and his proposal and headed west with him in a wagon. They were forced to trade the wagon for supplies before they ever got past Louisiana, and they made it into Austin's colony riding two horses and leading a packmule. Their luck had run to the same pattern ever since.

Though their marriage had been arranged more by mutual agreement than by any actual romance, she gradually developed a genuine affection for him, and he for her. If sometimes she looked at other young married couples and sensed a fire which her own marriage lacked, she tried not to let herself dwell upon the thought. Sure, life was hard. The country itself was hard. But surely there would be better times ahead. Surely luck would change. Anyway, she had observed that the fire of young love inevitably died down, and in doing so it often left the couple with a sense of loss and frustration. Better to have an affection that was genuine even if it never blazed. At least, Jim would always be there.

But Jim was not here, and he never would be again. As always, luck had run against him. Heather Winslow looked down upon the peaceful face of the sleeping boy and wished for that kind of peace. The terror still came to her, sometimes, in a nightmare. She could only hope it would fade . . . that she could forget the awful morning Jim Winslow had made his final sacrifice to let Heather go on to safety. Seeing the Mexican patrol catching up, knowing the two of them could never make the timber, he had given his protesting wife the fastest horse, kissed her goodbye and had ridden back with a rifle to hold up the patrol.

The firing had stopped about the time she reached the timber. Under cover of the trees, Heather had waited, praying desperately. When she saw the patrol come over the hill, she knew the outcome of the fight. She rode on alone, pushing all night, leaving the patrol far behind.

That one time, at least, Jim Winslow accomplished what he set out to do.

Heather Winslow could see Ocie Quitman now, riding the point position far out ahead of the wagons. He rode now as he always rode . . . alone. She remembered the way she had seen him the morning after Jim had died. Near exhaustion, the horse so tired he was barely walking, she had come out of the timber and into a clearing. A bewildered little boy had stood there by a wagon, and a man sat with his head in his hands beside a newly filled grave. Easing down from the saddle, she had reached Ocie Quitman before he even sensed that anyone was near. Looking up and seeing she was a woman, he had cried out, "Oh God, why couldn't you have come sooner?"

She had remembered him as being from the same general part of the colony, out on the Colorado. Brokenly he told her he had just buried his wife and a newborn son. The Runaway Scrape had killed her. It had been too much—the hard trip, the rough flight barely ahead of the Mexican army at the time for her delivery.

"There was no one to help her," Quitman had cried. "No one but me."

After a while, when he had time to think, he decided what to do. "My boy needs a woman's care. I need your horse, and you need my wagon. So you take the wagon, ma'am, and get my boy to the Sabine. I'll take the horse and catch up to Houston's army."

"How'll I get the boy back to you, and the wagon?"

"I'll find you. You stay put, the other side of the river. When the fightin' is over, I'll come and find you."

She had already seen what could happen to a man. "And if you *don't* come?"

"I got folks in the States. You can send the boy to them. And the wagon is yours." He gave her what little money he had and rode off across the valley and out of sight.

She never got across the Sabine. With hundreds of other refugees, she had been stranded on the Texas side by high water, within sound of the cannon at San Jacinto. The day after the cannons stopped, Ocie Quitman came.

All that was behind her now. She could not afford to dwell upon it too much. What mattered was the times that lay ahead. She hated to think of them, but she knew she must. The thought of operating the farm alone was staggering. She didn't know how she could do it all by herself. But what else could she do? Hire a man? With what? How could she pay him? All the cash money she owned in this world probably wouldn't add up to three dollars.

There was one possibility, of course, though even to think about it so early was brazen, and her conscience plagued her. She knew it must be considered shameful, her husband just a few weeks dead.

She could marry again.

Surely she would, in time. She was still a young woman, not yet even twenty-five. And though the years of hard work and frustration had left their mark on her face and on her hands, she knew she was still considered a comely woman. Not as pretty as some who hadn't been through so much toil and care, but still not bad to look upon. She was credited with being a right smart of a cook. And in this land where unattached women were far fewer than the men, she should not have to worry that she would be passed over unnoticed. She would have to wait a while, of course, for it would not be seemly to show interest in men so soon. And in the meantime there was the farm, and the problem of operating it. There was the problem of how she would live and how she would eat, how she would protect herself in this big, lonely, savage land where tranquillity and happiness stood always in jeopardy of being shattered in a few short moments of violence and terror.

If there had been anywhere else to go after the Scrape, she would never have started west again. But the grandparents were dead now. There had been nowhere else, unless she decided to cross over the Sabine and throw herself upon the pity of some unknown community that already had problems enough of its own, some community that did not know her and owed her nothing more than the impersonal charity which all mankind owes to the unfortunate. In the west, at least, she had the farm.

That was it, then. She would follow along and trust the Lord to mark the way. But she would keep her own eyes open, too. She always had.

Joshua Buckalew rode close to the wagons. Heather Winslow found herself looking at him often, wondering. He had told little, and all she could remember of him was once when he and the happy little man, Muley Dodd, had come by her cabin with the surveyor Jared Pounce. She smiled, remembering how Pounce had bragged about her corn dodgers. He'd been a great one for eating, old Pounce. And he had been fond of Buckalew, she remembered. That spoke well of him, for Pounce had been a shrewd judge of character.

Now Muley Dodd spent most of his time back with the youngsters and the stock. He came up once and took a long look at little Patrick, still asleep with his head on Heather's lap. Muley tipped his hat and smiled. "Sure do look peaceful, don't he, ma'am?"

She nodded and gave him back his smile. "He'll be with you again directly, when he gets his nap."

"Just wanted to be sure he was all right, ma'am. Didn't ever want to see him sick or nothin'."

Muley turned to ride back to the other youngsters. Heather Winslow's gaze followed him. Joshua Buckalew dropped back beside her wagon. "Muley's a good hand with kids, Mrs. Winslow. He'll take care of the boy."

"I'm glad you two came along. Little Patrick thinks the sun rises and sets with Muley."

The breeze carried the sound of Muley's tuneless whistling, as if there had never been any trouble in the world. Josh said, "Sometimes I think maybe it does. Times, I'd swap places with him and never look back."

"You've known him a long time?"

"Since back home in Tennessee. He needed a friend. So did I."

Her gaze found Ramón Hernandez, riding alone on one flank of the wagons. "And *him*?"

"We were neighbors. And we were friends, long before the war was ever thought of. We decided to stay friends, no matter what."

"Hasn't been easy, has it?"

"Been a strain. I lost my brother Thomas at Goliad. For a while it was hard for me to look at Ramón and see anything but his brown skin. But I had to get it through my head that he wasn't noway to blame for whatever Santa Anna did. I had to get it straight that I wasn't just lookin' at a Mexican . . . I was lookin' at an old friend. It wasn't him that had changed . . . it was the times." Josh frowned. "Ramón worries you, don't he?"

Heather nodded, her lips drawn tight as she glanced down at the sleeping boy. "I know better, but I can't help it. The feeling crawls over my skin every time I look at him. I know it wasn't his fault about my Jim, but the feeling is there, just the same."

"You tried to be kind, takin' him his supper, tryin' to save him from the treatment some of them would've given him in the cabin."

"Guilty conscience, I suppose. I knew I was doing him a wrong, and something inside of me was trying to make up for it. I hope he understands. I can't help the way I feel."

"He understands, ma'am."

Joshua Buckalew pulled away and drifted out toward Ramón Hernandez. Heather Winslow watched him from under the shadow of her bonnet, wondering what kind of farmer *he* was.

V

OCIE QUITMAN WAS RIDING POINT, UP AHEAD OF the wagons. In late afternoon he turned back, looking over his shoulder, his worried manner indicating something was wrong. Josh rode forward and met him abreast of the Provost wagon. Quitman spoke to Josh and Aaron Provost together. "Men up yonder a-horseback. Five or six, at least. Maybe more."

"Indians?" Josh asked.

"Not Indian, and from the looks of them I'd say probably not Mexican either. They're movin' in our direction."

Aaron squinted. "Could be settlers like us, on their way home."

"Possible. But if they was, they'd be movin' in a different direction. Unless, of course, they seen us and decided to come down and get acquainted." Quitman's hands moved restlessly on the rifle held across his lap.

Tensing, Josh reached down and brought up his own rifle. In the backwash of every war roam the scavengers feeding on other people's misery. In this one, that breed rode along behind the fleeing settlers during the Runaway Scrape, falsely telling them the Mexicans were about to catch up, then plundering the goods the frightened people dumped in their haste.

Rebecca Provost groaned. "Aaron, look how far the young'uns have dropped back." The children had allowed the loose stock to graze, and now they were at least a quarter mile behind. But Muley had come forward hungry, wanting to know how long it would be before they stopped to camp. He was still with the wagons.

Josh said urgently, "Muley, you go fetch them kids up here and do it in a hurry. Leave the stock. We can pick them up later. Get them kids to the wagons before those riders reach here."

Alarmed, Muley held back to ask questions. Impatiently Josh shouted, "Muley, I said move!" Muley spurred away, but he kept looking back.

Sessum and McAfee had lagged with their wagon, sulking all day since they had lost the chickens. Now they caught the excitement and saw the riders. They brought their team up in a hurry. Sessum's eyes were big with alarm. "What's happenin'?"

Provost said tightly, "We got company comin'."

Rebecca had stood up in the wagonbed, looking back worriedly toward the children. Heather Winslow had stopped her wagon, and Mrs. Provost was telling her about the horsemen. Aaron Provost threw out a question which didn't seem to be pointed at anybody in particular. "What do we do?"

Josh waited to see if anybody else said anything. "First thing is to see that every gun we got is loaded and in hand. Rifles, shotguns, whatever we have."

Wiley McAfee hadn't grasped the situation. "If they ain't Mexicans, and they ain't Indians, what we need to worry about? The war's over."

Quitman clipped, "Not everywhere, it ain't. See after your guns."

Josh quickly took inventory. He and Quitman each had a rifle. Provost had a shotgun, which probably was best because Josh suspected the farmer might have a bad case of buck fever if it came to a shooting. A shotgun was good insurance against bad marksmanship. McAfee and Sessum each had rifles. An extra rifle lay in the Provost wagon. It belonged to the oldest Provost boy, Daniel, but he was back yonder with the youngsters. Josh glanced in that direction, then once more at the approaching horsemen. It was too late. The kids weren't going to reach the wagons before the visitors did.

"Mrs. Provost," Josh said, "you better take charge of your son's rifle. You may have to use it."

"Lord, not me," she protested, fright beginning to show. "I can do lots of things, but I can't shoot a man."

"Have it ready, anyway," Quitman said.

Josh glanced back at Heather Winslow, who was watching the children, her fist balled against her mouth. Josh dug a Mexican pistol out of his blanket roll and loaded it. It was his first intention to hand it to Mrs. Winslow, but on second thought he doubted she would use it. Better he keep it, for he *would* use it.

The riders were close now, and he could tell that Quitman hadn't seen them all. There were nine. Josh totted up the odds and didn't like them. One of the riders peeled away from the rest and spurred out to intercept Muley and the youngsters. Josh felt his heart go down. Muley had a rifle with him, but he wouldn't use it.

Josh found Ramón watching the youngsters. He could read the thought in the Mexican's mind: ride to them.

"Forget it, Ramón. If they got mischief on their minds—and they act like it—they'd never let you live long enough to reach them kids. Sit tight. We'll need all our guns right here in a bunch."

The riders slowed to a trot, then to a walk. They ap-

proached in a ragged line, some carrying pistols, some
carrying rifles, one toting a Mexican *escopeta*. The man
who appeared to be the leader pulled a length ahead and
raised his hand to signal a halt. He moved a little closer, but
not close enough to reach.

"Howdy." A thin smile flitted briefly across his bearded
face. His eyes hungrily surveyed the wagons. "Nice outfit
you folks got here. Headin' west, I take it?"

Aaron Provost waited until he saw that neither Josh nor
Quitman seemed inclined to answer. "We're goin' back to
our homes. We understand the Mexican soldiers have all
gone. It's safe now."

The bearded man slouched lazily in his saddle. "Not altogether, it ain't. There's still a chance some stragglin'
Mexicans are left. And then there's always the Indians.
You-all think about the Indians? Man thinks he's got everything goin' on a nice downhill grade and then some
sneakin' Comanche goes and takes his hair. It ain't right,
good folks havin' to fret over things like that. So us boys
here, we have done gone and formed us a kind of a frontier
rifle company. We're here to kill any stray Mexicans and
Indians we come across and make this country safe for the
good folks." His gaze fell on Ramón. "This one here a prisoner of yours? We'd be right tickled to take care of him."

They were a dirty, unkempt, hungry-looking bunch, all
of them. Josh had seen their kind, and he thought he had
them pegged already: renegades operating out of the no-
man's territory known as the Redlands, that wild and law-
less region that lay between the Texas colonies and the
settled regions of Louisiana. These people turned their
hands to all sorts of mischief: smuggling, counterfeiting,
making bad whisky, stealing horses and waging a bloody
brand of banditry, preying on travelers who tried to use the
dim traces across western Louisiana and eastern Texas.
Stephen F. Austin had organized militia bands against them

and had driven them out of the colonies. But now, in the turmoil of Santa Anna's invasion and defeat, they were back again, straggling across Texas like roving, hungry wolves dogging the buffalo herds to pick up the weak and the unwary. They were as bad as the Comanches. Worse even than the Mexicans, for at least the Mexicans had considered that they had a cause.

Provost looked over his shoulder. "One of your men has stopped our children. I'd like to know what he done that for."

"That's Beau," came the smiling reply. "He's partial to young'uns." The smile faded. "Them is good-lookin' wagons. They're loaded too. Looks like you-all have come out of the war pretty good."

"Everything that's in these wagons is rightfully ours."

"I didn't go to make it look like we doubt you none. Anybody can tell, you're quality folks. What I'm gettin' to is, we're poor men, all of us. You can see that for yourselves. They ain't nobody payin' us nothin' or feedin' us nothin' for the protection we're givin' folks and their property. We got to live off of the land or starve. And starvin' ain't much to our likin', I'll guarantee."

Quitman asked, "Anybody authorize you to give all this . . . protection?"

"We're doin' it on our own. Not everybody can fight with old General Sam and git the glory of it. Some has got to do the dirty little jobs that don't rate even a thank-you or a howdy-do. We ain't complainin' none, but we figure you owe us, friends."

"Owe you what?" demanded Aaron Provost.

"Depends. Depends on what-all you got in them wagons."

He made a move toward the wagon which carried the widow Winslow. Ocie Quitman blocked him. "That's as far as you go, *friend*."

The black-bearded one darkened. "I don't believe you-all have quite understood the situation yet."

Josh said, "We understand it. You come to rob us."

"Not rob. *Rob* ain't a good word. *Commandeer* is better. Got a military ring to it, *commandeer* has. Sounds nice and legal too."

"There ain't nothin' legal about you," Josh declared. "You ain't militia. You probably never fired a shot at a Mexican, unless he was some helpless settler or stragglin' soldier you caught out by himself. You got nothin' comin' to you from us. If you're hungry, there's game enough around here. You got no call to starve."

The leader shrugged broad shoulders that stretched a ragged old black coat almost to the ripping point. Evidently the coat hadn't been made for him. Josh guessed he stole it from somebody. Somebody dead, more than likely. The man said, "We'd intended to handle this nice, but looks like you-all are bound and determined not to have it that way. So, we'll have it your way instead. You'll notice there's more of *us* than there is of you. And you'll remember we got one man down yonder close-herdin' that bunch of young'uns. Now, I sent old Beau on purpose, because he don't shrink from nothin', Beau don't. If I was to tell him to put his pistol up to some young'un's head and blow his brains out, he'd do it and not wink an eye. He's mean, Beau is."

Rebecca Provost cried out, and Heather Winslow's face went white.

The man nodded with satisfaction. "I do believe you-all are gettin' to see things the way I do. Women always seem to understand quicker'n men."

Shaken, Aaron Provost rubbed his whiskered chin. "What do you want from us?"

The dark-clad man slouched a little more, exuding an air

of victory. "Well now, we ain't sure till we see what you got. We find we're needin' a little bit of everything."

Josh knew that was what they would take. *Everything*.

Provost looked at Josh and Quitman, his eyes begging for help. He said to the renegade, "You let our young'uns come on up and join us. Then we'll talk to you."

"You'll talk a right smart better the way things is. Beau'll take good care of them."

Provost said, "We got to have a few minutes to talk this over."

"We'll give you a few minutes, then. Here's our proposition: you turn them wagons over to us and walk away from here. You get yourselves good and clear of the wagons and we'll let the kids come on up. Afoot, of course. We find we sure do need us some horses."

"You'll want our guns too," Josh said dryly.

"Naturally. We need more guns. How else we goin' to fight Mexicans and Comanches?" He started to rein the horse around. "We'll give you three minutes to talk it over. If you ain't made up your mind by then, I'll have to send a little message down to Beau. I'd sure hate to do that. Like I told you, Beau is mean."

He rode off a short distance, he and his men. Then they turned to watch. But at least it was too far for them to hear.

Quitman's face had darkened. "You thinkin' the same as me, Buckalew?"

Aaron Provost broke in gravely, "There ain't no thinkin' to be done. They outnumber us, and they got the kids. We can't take no risks with them young'uns."

Quitman's gaze went back to Josh. Josh said, "Years ago, when me and Muley and my brother Thomas were comin' to Texas from Tennessee, we ran into this kind of trouble over in the Redlands."

"What did you do?"

"We killed them before they could kill us. They was sure goin' to. And if we walk away from these wagons, we're all dead. Us *and* the kids. Don't you see, Aaron, they can't steal a bunch of slow wagons and leave us to tell about it. Too much risk of people findin' us before they've had time to get in the clear. Soon's they get us afoot and helpless, they'll kill us all and make out like it was Indians or Mexicans. It's the only thing they *could* do."

Provost repeated, "They got us outnumbered."

"Only by three, and they've sent one man down to the kids. That leaves two more men here than we got. Bad luck that your oldest boy and Muley both got cut off, but we got to make do without them."

Quitman glanced doubtfully at Ramón. "What about him? Can he shoot?"

"He can pick your teeth at fifty yards."

Quitman counted on his fingers. "If every one of us hits a man, that leaves two of them alive here and us with empty rifles. Chances are one or maybe both of them will turn tail and run."

Incredulous, Aaron demanded, "You mean we're just goin' to shoot them down? That don't hardly seem Christian."

"What they're figurin' on doin' to us ain't Christian, either," Josh pointed out. "And remember, they'll do it to the women and the children same as us. Your damned right we'll shoot them down." He remembered that other time, in the Redlands. He'd had the same feeling as Provost then, but Thomas had been older and tougher. Thomas had made him see it through. Looking back afterwards Josh had realized it was the only way. Hard, even brutal. But you don't make deals with a hungry wolf. You may bribe him off so long as you keep feeding him, but when you've nothing else to give him, he'll take you.

Dent Sessum and Wiley McAfee had pulled their wagon in close so they could listen. Cold sweat broke out on their faces. Any enmity between them and Josh was momentarily shoved away in the face of this outside threat. Sessum asked, "What if two or three of us shoot at the same man?"

Quitman replied, "We got to parcel them out. McAfee, you get the one with that Mexican-lookin' sombrero. Aaron can shoot the one with the beaver hat. Hernandez'll take the one sittin' next to him, the one with the crooked neck that looks like he'd been hung and cut down early. Buckalew can take the one on the end, and I'll get the man that done all the talkin'."

Ramón had kept quiet. Now he motioned back down the trail toward the youngsters. Normally he spoke in Spanish, but now he had to force himself into broken English that came hard for him. "The children. That *hombre* Beau. Somebody got to shoot Beau."

Quitman frowned. "I was figurin' him for Sessum. From where you're at, Sessum, you got the best chance to shoot Beau. You can rest your rifle barrel across that stack of goods and draw a fine bead."

That would leave three men here alive, even if everybody hit his target.

Provost was murmuring, "I sure as sin don't like it."

Josh said, "What they got in mind, you'd like a lot less. Everybody better shoot straight. Kill them the first shot and you won't have anything to do over."

The three minutes passed, and the scavengers closed in, fanning out to form a semi-circle. Every one of them carried a gun of some kind, and every gun was ready. The only thing Josh figured his group could count on was the renegades' conviction that this was to be easy pickings, that the settlers would give up.

That, he thought, *gives us a couple seconds jump on them, because at least we know what we're going to do.*

The leader was coming close to the wagons, so sure was he of surrender. That would make an easy shot for Quitman, anyway. Josh let his attention settle then on the man at the end who was to be his target. He hoped the man wouldn't see it in his eyes.

Josh had shot a few men in the war, and he'd always wondered about it afterwards . . . who they were, where they had come from, how it came that they were destined to be at that particular place at that particular moment and to die by his hand rather than someone else's. It wasn't a pleasant thing to dwell on, after the bloody task was done. It was even less pleasant to dwell on *before* the deed. All he could see in the flesh was a wind-reddened face, a heavy cover of dirty whiskers streaked by tobacco, a set of pale eyes that found Josh's and stayed there. That and a pair of rough hands gripping a rifle that he intended to use for killing. Josh wondered if he had a family back home . . . a wife, maybe, and even some kids who would always wonder what had become of him, kids who would grow up wild and unrestrained and perhaps turn out in his own cruel image, not wholly at fault because they had known no other way. And was it really even *this* man's fault that he was here now, about to die but not knowing it? Had a careless fate pointed him in this direction when he was too young to understand? Josh would always wonder, but there would never be any way for him to know.

The men were so close now that he knew he could not miss. Cold sweat made the rifle slick in his hands. He felt the man must see the tension drawing his face tight, and he hoped it would be taken for fear.

"You made up your minds yet?" the leader asked casually.

"We have," Quitman replied. He waited a moment, then shouted, "NOW!"

Six weapons roared. Horses plunged and squealed. Men shrieked and cursed and fell. Through a cloud of black powdersmoke drifting out from the wagons, Josh watched his man jerk backward, clutching his stomach, then slide off and crumple in an awkward heap. Another man crawled on the ground, screeching, going limp as a terrified horse trampled him. The smoke was heavy, but Josh could see that at least four men had been left untouched. Someone had completely missed his target.

The fusillade had caught the renegades by surprise. Two of the ones not hit wheeled their horses and ran, coattails flapping as they spurred in panic. Josh saw a rifle flash from one of the two men who were left, but he didn't turn to see if one of his party was hit. He kicked his horse and moved quickly through the smoke, drawing the pistol out of his waistband. Ocie Quitman swung his riflebarrel, clubbing one rider out of the saddle. Josh saw the other one holding the *escopeta,* trying to find a target in the gray smoke. Josh brought up the pistol and squeezed the trigger. The man went down.

He heard Wiley McAfee scream, "Help me, somebody. He's got me!"

Josh wheeled. On the wagonseat, Aaron Provost sat frozen, the smoking shotgun in his hands, as he stared in hypnotic dismay at the renegade in the beaver hat, writhing on the ground. This was probably the first man Provost had ever shot.

On the far side of the wagon, Wiley McAfee and one of the Redlanders rolled in the grass. A knifeblade caught the sunshine for an instant. McAfee had failed to kill his man, and now he was fighting for his life.

Josh remembered the extra rifle in the Provost wagon, the one that belonged to the oldest boy. He made a move, but Ramón had thought of it before him. Ramón was closer, and he got to it first.

McAfee saw him, for he was shrieking, "Help me, Mexican! Help before he kills me!" He had never even bothered to learn Ramón's name.

Ramón climbed out of his saddle and onto the Provost wagon, moving awkwardly because of his bad leg. He grabbed the rifle, and for a moment Josh thought he was going to shoot the renegade who had McAfee down. But Ramón brought the rifle to a level and propped it across a box to fire it. Josh saw then what he was aiming at.

Sessum had missed his shot at the man called Beau. Now Beau pursued the little Provost girl, evidently trying to gain a hostage.

McAfee screamed again, "For God's sake, help before he kills me!"

But Ramón ignored him. Beads of sweat broke on the dark forehead as the barrel followed the moving Beau. The rifle roared. Beau slumped, grabbing at his horse's mane. In an instant Provost's oldest boy and Muley together had pounced on him and dragged him to the ground.

Josh ran to help McAfee. He was too late. The renegade plunged the knife into McAfee's throat. Quitman got there first. He leaned down from his saddle and jabbed the butt of his empty rifle savagely against the renegade's head. The man went slack, and Quitman clubbed him again. The skull broke like a melon.

Josh hadn't seen Sessum all this time, but now the man came running, eyes big as a washtub. "Wiley! What's happened, Wiley? Wiley!"

Wiley McAfee lay gasping, struggling as his lifeblood spread a stain in the grass. His hands reached up in fearful supplication, but no one could help him.

Sessum crouched over him a moment in shock, then grabbed up McAfee's fallen rifle and frenziedly began to club the fallen renegade.

Quitman said, "Sessum, that won't help none. He's already dead."

Sessum shouted, "I heard Wiley holler to the Mexican for help. Why didn't he help him?" His gaze fastened on Ramón, and he gripped the rifle barrel as if to use the weapon for a club. "Answer me, Mexican! How come you didn't help him? You wanted him dead!"

"The children," Ramón gritted. "McAfee was a man. First came the children."

Sessum seemed not to hear him. "You had a rifle in your hands, and you stood there and let him die."

Ramón shrugged. He'd made his explanation. Sessum could accept it, or he could go to hell.

Josh put in, "Sessum, it was your job to shoot Beau. You missed him and left them young'uns in his hands. Ramón had to finish your job." Pausing, he saw no sign that his words were taking any effect. "If you'd done what you was supposed to, McAfee would not have had to die."

Sessum gave no indication he had even heard. "That Mexican could've saved him. He let him be killed." Sessum made a move forward with the rifle barrel gripped in his hands. Josh caught him by the shoulder, spun him around and struck him on the chin. Sessum sprawled. Josh picked up the fallen rifle to keep it out of Sessum's hands.

Over the hill he could see two men riding away, still spurring. The wise thing would be to go after them, to make sure the whole den was killed out. But here with the smoke still thick enough to choke a man, and with the dying men groaning on the ground and women sobbing softly in the wagons, he was glad to let them go.

Muley and the oldest Provost boy rode up with the children, and with the wounded Beau staggering at the end of a rope.

Muley said quickly in self defense, "There wasn't nothin' I could do, Josh. He taken my rifle before I even knowed what was goin' on."

Josh looked at the captured man. "You did fine, Muley. So did you, Daniel."

The Provost boy sat straight and proud, though he trembled from the excitement. "We wasn't afraid of him, Mister Buckalew. Quick as we got the chance, we grabbed onto him."

Muley shouted, "He was fixin' to kill the children. That's what he told us. Said if anything went wrong he was goin' to kill them off one by one, like he'd wring chicken necks. He was tryin' to catch the girl when somebody shot him."

Quitman's eyes were sharp. He told Beau: "Your friends are dead, most of them. You know any reason we ought to have mercy on you?"

"I'm bleedin' to death," Beau whined. "You can't let a man stand here and bleed to death."

"No," said Quitman, "we can't." He squeezed the trigger. Beau jerked, stared in horror till his eyes went blank, then he pitched forward in a heap.

Quitman said to no one in particular, "That's what he was fixin' to do to the young'uns." He switched his gaze to Josh. "What you waitin' for? Any others still alive, we better do the same to them. No use them healin' up and pullin' this on somebody else."

Josh said, "We're not the law."

"Aren't we? There ain't no law right now except the law we make. Mexican government is gone. We got no Texas government except on paper."

"There's still God's law."

"God ain't come west of the Sabine River."

"You're not goin' to kill anybody else, Quitman."

"You figure on stoppin' me?"

"If I have to."

Quitman's gaze could cut steel. All Josh knew was to stare back. They watched each other like buck deer trying to decide whether to lower their horns and fight. Finally Quitman shrugged. "You could take lessons from that Mexican of yours. He knows when to let his blood run cold."

Provost came out of his daze and climbed shakily down from his wagon. They all scouted around, picking up the guns and looking over the blood-soaked renegades, scattered in a grisly semi-circle where they had fallen. It would have been a sickening sight, had Josh not already seen so many others, most of them worse. The man Josh had shot with the pistol lay breathing raggedly, already unconscious. He would never open his eyes. The rest appeared dead except the one who had worn the beaver hat. The hat lay crushed beneath him. Provost had shot him, but nervousness had spoiled his aim. The blue whistlers had shattered the leg.

Quitman said, "Leave him be and he'll bleed to death."

This one, of all the renegades, showed no whiskers. Bending over for a close look, Josh exclaimed: "He's a young'un, is all. Not much older than Daniel Provost. Seventeen . . . maybe eighteen."

Quitman frowned. "A young'un can kill you as dead as an old one. He's part of that trash."

"He's not old enough to know what he's doin'."

"The hell he ain't. He's old enough to kill a man. That means he's old enough for somebody to kill *him* and not worry over it none."

Searching the lad, Josh found a knife but no other weapon. He slit the shot-torn trouser leg. The youngster choked off a cry. Josh grimaced. "Busted into little bitty pieces. We got to do somethin'."

Quitman growled, "Leave him."

"He's just a kid."

"We was all kids, one time or another. I knew right from wrong by the time I was six. He's growed up with a wolf-pack, Buckalew. You can't change a wolf's habits. Save him now and he'll kill again. Leave him die. It's best for everybody."

"We can't."

"While ago you helped me plan how we'd kill them all. It didn't bother you then."

"He had a gun in his hands. Now it's different. He's helpless."

"You think he'd of fixed *you* up? He'd of cut your throat."

Aaron Provost said, "Ocie, it was me that shot him. We got to give him a chance."

Quitman shrugged. "Do it then. But remember, if you save him he'll like as not be at your throat first chance he gets."

Josh looked to Muley for help, but Muley's face was clabber-white at the sight of so much blood. "Muley, you gather the young'uns and take them to the shade of that tree yonder to wait and rest. No use them bein' here at this slaughterhouse."

Still shaken, Aaron Provost said, "I'll help you with the boy, Josh. I feel like it's my responsibility. What you want me to do?"

"Let's take a better look at this wound." Josh ripped away the trouser leg, his brow furrowing. It was even worse than he thought. A chill crawled up his back. Looking away, he saw that Aaron's boy Daniel had taken it upon himself to round up the renegades' horses. Nobody had had to tell him. And Josh remembered how Daniel had pounced on Beau the moment Ramón's rifleball struck. Good boy, that Daniel. Aaron and Rebecca had pointed him right. Pity there hadn't been somebody to point *this* boy right. "Aaron, why don't you look through them saddlebags and find out if any of them had a bottle of whisky or somethin'? This boy is goin' to need it. He's goin' to need aplenty of it."

Josh made a tourniquet of the trouserleg, then walked to the widow Winslow's wagon where Ocie Quitman had his arms around his little son Patrick. "Mrs. Winslow, could you get a fire goin' and heat some water, please? We're goin' to need it directly."

Aaron found a couple of bottles. Josh removed the stopper from one and tilted it up to drink. He gasped and wiped his sleeve across his mouth. "Man who'd sell that stuff would club his grandmother. But it'll do the job. Here, boy, drink. Drink it all."

By the time the water was boiling, the boy was floating away in a drunken stupor. Josh had whetted his knife until the blade was keen. He held it in the boiling water, glanced at Aaron and said, "You hold him."

The boy surged against Aaron, screaming, then fell back in a faint. Cold sweat broke out on Josh's forehead. Once he turned away to be sick. But he came back, and presently the job was done. Heather Winslow fled while Josh and Aaron cauterized the stump. Then she forced herself forward with some homespun cotton cloth. "You'll need bandages."

Quitman and Dent Sessum had placed Wiley McAfee's body in the Sessum wagon. Josh walked up to Quitman. "We got to put that boy in a wagon too. We want to use yours."

Quitman frowned. "What if I said no?"

"You and me would have to fight. And when it was over, we'd put the boy in your wagon anyhow."

Quitman shook his head in resignation. "You got a soft heart, Buckalew, and a soft head to match. Like as not, it'll

get you killed someday. But go ahead. If it's all right with
Mrs. Winslow, you can use the wagon."

They put a couple of miles behind them, leaving the battlefield with the bodies lying where they had fallen. They
camped on a little creek beneath a canopy of freshly-leafed
pecan trees. Josh and Muley and Aaron gathered old leaves
into a soft mat, spread blankets and placed the wounded
boy on them. The lad was groaning.

Dent Sessum and Ocie Quitman carried shovels up to a
high point and dug a grave for Wiley McAfee. After supper, Aaron read from the Bible, they all bowed their heads,
and each man took a turn with the shovel.

Josh watched Sessum carve McAfee's name onto a cross
Muley had fashioned. He suspected Sessum had mis-
spelled the name, but he saw no need in making an issue of
it. He asked, "Did McAfee have any relatives you know of?
Is there somebody we ought to send a letter to?"

Sessum shook his head. "We was partners, him and me.
There wasn't nobody else."

"Bound to be somebody . . . a mother, maybe, or a sister
or brother . . . somebody who ought to get the stuff that belonged to him."

Sessum put aside the cross and clenched his fists, his
face darkening. "We was partners. Whatever belonged to
him belongs to me now. Everything in that wagon, it belongs to me. Just me! You ain't goin' to take away or give
away what's mine!"

"I had no intention . . ."

"I'm warnin' you, Buckalew. Touch one thing on that
wagon and there'll be big trouble. It's all mine now, do you
hear?"

Josh turned away, disgust welling in him. He picked up a
shovel and started toward the wagon. Aaron Provost
trudged out to meet him, his shoulders slumped, his face
grim. "Don't put the shovel away, Josh."

"The boy?"

The farmer's voice broke. "He died fightin'."

Somberly Josh pondered the waste and the futility of it all. At length he made a Mexican shrug of resignation. "At least we tried."

Anguished, Aaron cried, "It was me that shot him, Josh. How am I goin' to carry that burden? He was a boy like my Daniel."

"No, Aaron, not like your boy. This one was suckled on wolf's milk, taught to kill like an animal. It wasn't your fault. The blame goes on the people who raised him that way."

VI

THE DAYS WERE LONG AND THE MILES PASSED
slowly under the wheels, but gradually the Spanish
moss country of the coastal lands fell behind them and the
gently rising prairies marked the way into the higher, dryer
inland regions of Texas ... across the Brazos, past the
charred ruins of Stephen F. Austin's San Felipe, across the
San Bernard and finally west to the Colorado.

Ocie Quitman had never talked much, and as the wagons
rolled farther west he said even less than before. He rode
ahead, alone, a morose silence gathered about him like
some dark cloud. Now and again Josh spoke to him and re-
ceived no answer, for Quitman's mind was somewhere far
away.

Aaron Provost said, "We're gettin' close to home country now, to the place we all called Hopeful Valley. I'm right
uneasy, Josh, how he's goin' to take it when he first sets
eyes on his farm. You can tell, lately he's done a lot of
thinkin' about *her*."

The farther they moved across the prairies, the more uneasy Josh became about Comanches. The only horse tracks
they had encountered crossing their trail had proved to be

bands of wild mustangs, grazing free. While Quitman rode his solitary point, Josh and Ramón would each move far out on the flank, watching. They stirred up deer, which would bound away in long, fleet leaps. Sometimes antelope raced across the prairie ahead of them, their white-puff tails bobbing. The riders found wild cattle, a few of which they promptly brought in for beef. But they saw no Indians, and no sign of any.

A day came when Quitman rode forward to the top of a hill and sat his horse there unmoving. After a long time Josh became uneasy and loped up from his flank position. From on the other side, he could see Ramón follow his lead. At the hilltop, Josh stopped and looked down upon a small field, evidently plowed last winter but now growing up in weeds. His searching gaze picked up a small, crooked stream, its green banks lined with massive pecan trees. Finally, just above the stream, he saw the black skeleton of a cabin, the charred logs of its tumbled walls spread out like burned ribs.

He knew with a cold certainty. "Your place?"

Quitman made no answer. Josh thought he had never seen a face so sad. He held his silence, studying the place. He could tell it had been a good farm. It would be again, with some work. "Cabin's easy to build," he offered finally. "Soon's we all get our field work caught up with, we'll help you put it back up."

Quitman shook his head. "Cabin don't mean nothin' to me. Mary is what mattered, and there ain't no way to bring her back."

Josh thought, *A man has to put his dead behind him and go on living*. But he figured it would sound cruel, no matter how he said it.

Quitman pointed at the remains of the cabin. "It wasn't much, but she loved it there. Had her some flowers in front of it, and her garden out back, where you see that square plot with the log fence. I remember how aggravated she'd

get when the coons would come slippin' in at night and tear
the garden up. She'd take a broom and chase them out—
she wouldn't hurt one for the world. Then she'd go out next
mornin' and try to fix the damage. She could make anything grow, Mary could. She had the touch of life about
her. She could take a sick plant or a sick animal or a sick
bird—didn't matter which—and she could make it live."
His eyes pinched. "But when her own time come, she
couldn't help herself. Whatever touch she had, it wouldn't
work for *her*."

"It was a hard go of luck, but I reckon there wasn't anything anybody could do."

Quitman gave a quick, hard glance at Ramón. "There
was somebody could've done somethin', but they wouldn't."
His head turned slowly, and Josh followed his gaze south-
ward. He thought he saw a wisp of light-colored smoke beyond the trees. He glanced at Quitman, but he didn't ask
the question.

Quitman's voice was barbed. "Faustino Marquez." His
hands balled into fists. He stared toward the thin column of
smoke, his face darkening. Finally he said, "Buckalew, you
want to do me a favor?"

Josh frowned, dubious. "If I can."

"Come along with me, then. I want you to stand back
and keep quiet. I don't want you to interfere or get in the
way of whatever I do except for one thing. The last second
before I kill him, I want you to stop me. Let me burn him
out. Let me beat him to within an inch of his life. But don't
let me kill him."

"I don't know . . ." Josh rubbed his jaw. "Before I'm a
party to this, I better know how come you hate him so bad."

Quitman turned to Ramón. "I'd rather *you* didn't go with
us."

Ramón glanced at Josh, his eyes asking. Josh said, "It's

all right, Ramón. I'll go with him. Maybe you better go help watch out for the wagons anyway."

Quitman touched heels to his horse's ribs and started down the hill toward the smoke. Josh hurried to follow.

"Quitman, you didn't answer me."

Without slowing his horse, Quitman painfully spilled out his story. "Time I'm finished, you'll know why I can't stand the sight of a Mexican. Not even that pet of yours. Faustino Marquez as good as killed my wife. He could've saved her, but he wouldn't lift a hand." Quitman spat. "Two years, we was neighbors. Faustino was the hungry kind, never satisfied with what he had, takin' everything else he could get. A grasper. Whatever he needed, he come borrowin' from us, and I'd have hell gettin' it back. But the times him or his wife got sick, Mary would go over and take care of them. The big fever come last year. Mary stayed there most of a week, nursin' Alicia Marquez, pullin' her back after the fever all but took her away. Faustino swore if there was ever anything Mary needed, he'd give up his life to help her.

"Well, the time come. We had another baby on the way when the war commenced. I went off to help fight. After the Alamo and Goliad, when the Scrape started, I got leave to go home and see after Mary. All our *Americano* friends had packed up and left. They'd tried to get Mary to go with them, but she'd waited for me. I got home and found her so close to her time that it was dangerous for her to travel. Santa Anna's Mexicans was almost on top of us by then. I was afraid ridin' in a wagon would kill her.

"Bein' Mexicans themselves, Faustino and his wife didn't see no need in them runnin' from Santa Anna. I decided that if Mary stayed with the Marquez family, the soldiers wouldn't bother her none, so I put her and Patrick in the wagon and took them over there. Faustino met me at the door with a gun in his hand. Said for us damned *Americanos* to get off of his land. I told him he owed Mary protection, but he said if we didn't get away, he'd shoot us all and maybe Santa Anna would give him a medal. Said this land was for the Mexicans anyway, and the only reason they'd ever let any *Americanos* in here in the first place was to help them fight off the Comanches. Said our place was *his* place from now on.

"We rode all that day and through the night and hid in a thicket at daylight. It kept rainin' and washin' our tracks out behind us. While we was in the thicket, a bunch of Mexican soldiers come ridin' by, tryin' to find us. And up front, helpin' them, was Faustino Marquez." Ocie Quitman's eyes closed. "We traveled by night and hid by day. But it turned out like I was afraid it would. Mary's time came, and the trip had been too much for her. She died hard. The baby never drew a breath. I reckon you know the rest of it."

Josh said, "Heather Winslow told me."

"Mrs. Winslow was in a lot the same shape as I was. She'd lost her husband, and I'd lost my wife. I gave her Patrick and the wagon and went on to find Sam Houston. I'd made up my mind to kill as many Mexicans as I could. And I did, Buckalew. I made them pay."

"But it wasn't enough, was it?"

Quitman shook his head. "No, it wasn't enough. All the time I knew Faustino was still here. I laid awake nights, thinkin' about all the slow, hard ways I could use to kill him. None of them was good enough. Once he was dead, he wouldn't feel anything, and I wanted him to feel. Then I got to thinkin' about how greedy he was. I decided the way to punish him most was to run him off of his place with nothin' but the shirt on his back and let him spend the rest of his miserable life rememberin' what he had thrown away. That's a way you can kill a man and still leave him alive."

"That's what you want me to help you do?"

"Not help me. I'll do it all myself. You just be there to make sure I don't forget myself and kill him. Agreed?"

Josh hesitated. "I reckon you got cause enough to hate him. But I'll stop you whenever I think it's time."

The Marquez house lay beyond a recently-tilled field. It was of stone, Mexican style, rather than the log type the *Americano* settlers favored. Smoke curled from the chimney, and Josh thought he saw movement inside. No one came out. Quitman's eyes narrowed.

"Faustino!"

No answer.

"Faustino! You drag yourself out here, and be damned quick!"

A broad-hipped Mexican man showed himself uncertainly in the open doorway. He stared at Quitman with the horrified eyes of a man who has seen the dead spring to life. "Quitman!"

Ocie Quitman carried his rifle across the pommel of his saddle. His voice was quieter now but keen-edged. "Thought they'd got me, didn't you? Thought I'd never come back." Quitman's gaze swept over the yard. It fastened on a plow, and his eyes crackled. "That's *my* plow you got. And that chair under the arbor . . . it's one I made for Mary."

Marquez stammered. "All this I save for you, Quitman. I say to myself, that Santa Anna, he burn everything. I bring it over here, and I save it for my good friend Quitman and his wife." He trembled. "I save it for you, Quitman."

"You stole it. You didn't think I'd be back."

"No, Quitman, I no steal from you. You and me, we friends."

"So friendly you led the Mexican troops to try and find

us? You wanted us dead, Faustino. You wanted to steal everything for yourself."

"Long time we are friends," Marquez quailed. "You and me, your wife, my Alicia. Do you forget that?"

"*You're* the one that forgot it." Quitman swung down slowly, the rifle's muzzle pointing in Marquez's general direction. Marquez began shrinking back inside the door.

"Faustino! You stay out here or I'll put a bullet in you!"

The Mexican slumped, stricken with fear. "Please, you don't kill me, Quitman. Please."

"You killed my Mary. Why shouldn't I kill you?"

"I did nothing."

"You did nothin', and that is why she's dead. You owed her a debt, but you let her die. Now I owe *you,* Faustino, and I'm goin' to pay."

The butt of his rifle caught Marquez in the stomach. The man bent forward, arms coming around instinctively for protection. Quitman jabbed the butt straight forward, hitting him again. Marquez stumbled backward into the house. A woman screamed. Josh dismounted, looped the reins through the brush fence and moved quickly through the open door. He saw a plump Mexican woman cowering in a corner, face covered with her hands, but her fingers spread enough that she could see. Each time Quitman hit her husband, she screamed. An old rifle stood in another corner, but neither she nor Marquez made any move toward it. Josh picked it up and took it out of contention.

What Quitman did to Marquez was slow, methodical and brutal. He drove him back against a stone wall and there proceeded to beat him with his fists. Each time Marquez slipped to the packed-earth floor, Quitman hauled him up again. Marquez made only a small attempt to defend himself. He whimpered and pleaded that he did not want to die.

About the time Josh was preparing to step in and stop it,

Quitman flung Marquez halfway across the room. "Get up, Faustino. Get up and get out!"

Marquez pushed himself up onto hands and knees, staring without comprehension. *"No entiendo." I do not understand.*

"I said get out. You and your wife, get your oxen and hook up your *carreta* and go. Don't you ever come back."

The woman spoke for the first time. Up to now, all she had done was scream. "This is our home."

"It *was* your home. You're leavin'."

"Where?" she pleaded in Spanish. "We have nowhere to go."

Quitman strode across the room and hauled Marquez to his feet. "You hear me, Faustino?" The man nodded in terror. Quitman said, "If I was you I wouldn't stop till I got plumb the other side of the Rio Grande. Don't stop in Bexar, because I might go there sometime. Don't stop at the Neuces, because I might be *there* sometime too. I promise you this, Faustino: if I ever see you again . . . any time, any place . . . I'll kill you on sight!" He turned loose. The Mexican fell to his hands and knees, scrambling for the door, not pushing to his feet until he was outside. The woman began gathering up clothes and cooking utensils. Quitman raised his hand. "Leave them."

She stared in disbelief.

He repeated, "Leave them. I'm givin' you Faustino. That's all you're leavin' here with."

Josh said: "You're makin' it awful tough. How're they goin' to live?"

"That's their problem. They didn't give a damn what happened to Mary."

Josh watched somberly as the Mexican yoked his oxen to a high-wheeled wooden cart. The couple left without so much as the old rifle.

Josh said, "They might run into Comanches."

"They might."

"They'd have no chance at all."

"They'd have all the chance they gave Mary." Quitman turned back inside the little rock house. The anger still rode high in his face. "Damn near everything in here—the chairs, the table, all of it—came from our house. Faustino cleaned it out. Then he burned it."

"So now you've cleaned him out."

"Clean as a hound's tooth."

Quitman walked toward the homemade wooden bed. Josh guessed by the way he looked at it that it had been his—his and Mary's. Quitman picked up a pillow and let his fingers run over the fine embroidery work, and he turned away, his head down. Josh decided to leave the cabin and give the man his moments of peace . . . if ever he had any.

They rode in silence across the field and over the hill to Quitman's own place. Quitman moved his horse in a slow walk around the rock pens, the burned cabin, the weed-grown garden. He kept his eyes away from Josh's, and Josh tried not to intrude. He held back, willing to listen if it would help but not wanting to put himself in where he wasn't needed.

At length Quitman reined up, shoulders slumped. "I don't think I can do it, Buckalew."

"Do what?"

"Live here again. I could come here and work the land, maybe, but I couldn't live here anymore. There's too much that'd try to take me back, and there's no goin' back. Like as not, I'd go out of my mind."

"What do you think you'll do?"

"Texas owes me free land for my soldierin'. Didn't you say there's good land up your way?"

Josh nodded. "There's a lot that ain't been claimed."

"Then I'll pick me a piece of it bye and bye and put in my claim. This place I'll keep for my boy Patrick."

"You'll be welcome." Josh frowned. "There's just one thing . . ."

"What's that?"

"You'll have Mexican neighbors again. You'll have Ramón Hernandez. It won't be like it was with Faustino. Push Ramón and he'll fight. What's more, I'll help him."

Quitman stared at him unflinchingly. "I got a notion I'll have to fight you sooner or later anyhow."

VII

HEATHER WINSLOW HAD THOUGHT SHE WOULD BE prepared to face the sight of her burned-out home, for she had seen enough others along the way to know she could expect nothing else. But the tears came anyway as she stared at the cold, blackened chimney which towered as a silent sentinel over a pile of charred logs.

Gaunt Rebecca Provost stood behind her, strong hands gripping Heather's shoulders. "Go ahead, child, cry if it'll help you any. But there's plenty more logs where them come from. The men'll put you up another one. All it takes is time and labor and some good timber. You'll have you a home again."

It will take more to make this a home, Heather thought. *Without Jim, there will be no man in the house. And without a man in the house, it won't be a home.*

She heard a quiet voice which she knew belonged to Joshua Buckalew. "Mrs. Provost is right. First thing we got to do is see after the crops, includin' yours. Then we'll get to work buildin' the cabins back the way they was, or better, even. We'll put a good roof over your head, you don't need to be worryin' about that."

Aaron Provost declared confidently, "Bound to be one of us has a cabin that didn't get burned. We'll all stay together till we know it's safe for us to break off on our own. If Rebecca and me has been lucky, you'll share our house, Heather. You'll share it as long as you need it."

But the Provosts hadn't been lucky either. Their big double cabin lay in black ruins, even one of its two tall chimneys broken off and lying in a heap of rubble.

Heather was not much surprised to see a lone tear roll down Rebecca Provost's tight-stretched cheek, nor was she surprised to see the tall woman square her shoulders and jut her chin forward, shutting off the tears like she would shutter and bar a window.

Aaron Provost's eyes were grim. "Where to from here? Think your cabin might still be standin', Josh?"

Josh shook his head. "It was already burned the last time I came this way. Indians, I figured. No use us goin' by there."

Sitting on his horse, Ocie Quitman shook his head in resignation. "Then there's noplace else. We'd just as well set up camp here."

Josh said, "Wrong. There's still Ramón's. It's a good ways from Hopeful Valley, but I know the place will still be there. His family stayed. Be all right with you, Ramón, if we set up camp there till we get everybody's fields plowed out and the cabins rebuilt?"

Ramón nodded. "We would be happy."

Ocie Quitman's gaze fixed itself on the Mexican. "You don't need to be doin' us no favors."

Ramón shrugged. "Would you not do the same for me?"

Quitman looked away, not answering. Heather thought she knew the answer, and she suspected Ramón knew it too. She wondered if Hernandez might purposely be twisting the knife a little.

Josh said, "They got a good rock house that the Indians have never tried to hit. It'd be a safe place for the women and children till we find out about the Comanches. We can't afford to go scatterin' right now anyway before we know how much of a hazard the Indians will be."

Quitman glared at Ramón. "I've always been careful who I let myself owe favors to."

Heather looked for resentment in Ramón's eyes, but if it was there he kept it well concealed. He said, "You owe me nothing. It is protection for my family if all of you go there. Everything is even."

Ocie did not yield. "I won't be beholden. I'll pay you out of my crops this fall. There ain't goin' to be no debt."

Ramón shrugged. *"No le hace."*

Josh looked at Dent Sessum. "How do you feel about it?"

Sessum glowered, not liking the situation but accepting it sourly. "I'll go along with whatever the majority wants. But I'll tell you this: I think if I help provide protection, that's pay enough. I ain't payin' that Mexican no extry."

Ramón repeated, "Nobody owes me."

Muley Dodd grinned happily. "Does that mean we're goin' to Ramón's now, Josh? Does that mean we're goin' to see all them Hernandez kids?"

Josh smiled. "And your old dog Hickory, too."

Muley rubbed his hands together, laughing. "Lordy, Josh, I'd almost forgot old Hickory. Bet he'll be right tickled to see us come. I can't hardly wait to go huntin' with him again."

Josh placed his hand on Muley's shoulder. Heather watched, admiring Buckalew for the friendship and the sense of duty which held him to the smaller man. Muley Dodd was like a child, she had realized from the first time she saw him. His heart was good and his intentions were honest, but an adolescent helplessness held him dependent upon Joshua Buckalew. She suspected that at times Muley must be burden enough to make a man weep.

If he's gentle like that with Muley, he'd be even gentler with a woman, she thought.

Jim had been gentle. In that respect he had been like Buckalew. Yet in other ways he'd been a bit like Muley Dodd, too. Not slow-thinking, the way Muley was, but somehow dependent, unsure. He had leaned on Heather for strength and she had tried to give it, even when she was stricken with anxiety herself.

Heather stared at Buckalew, then at Ocie Quitman. She doubted that either man ever leaned on anybody. They were strong men, self-confident, able to stand on their own feet and well aware of it. Either one of them would make a woman a good home. *Either one would make me a good home,* she told herself. Again she felt a touch of shame for this errant direction her thoughts were taking. It didn't seem there had been proper time yet for her to begin measuring other men as candidates to take Jim's place. But, then, these were not normal times, and this was not the settled homeland of her girlhood where the old rules could be applied without question. Out here a woman alone was a woman in jeopardy.

Well, she wouldn't be brazen about it. She would observe the amenities of widowhood and show all the proper respect. But she had to be realistic about the facts of the situation. The facts were that she was alone and couldn't afford to remain that way indefinitely. So she would watch and weigh and compare. When time had erased the obligations of propriety, and when Jim's face quit coming back unbidden in her dreams, she would know which man—if either—she wanted. And she would get him.

The most direct way to the Hernandez place did not include Joshua Buckalew's land, but it passed within a few miles of there. Heather could see nervousness building in Buckalew until he could stand it no longer.

"Aaron," he told the big farmer, "I just got to ride over and take a look. I'll catch up to you later."

He rode off over the hill, Muley Dodd spurring desperately to catch up. For hours Heather found herself watching, hoping to see them. At last they came, and she smiled a little, relieved. But she stopped smiling when she saw the sober expression in Buckalew's face. She asked no questions. She sat impatiently on the wagonseat and listened for Aaron Provost to do the asking.

"Burned out, was you, Josh?"

He nodded. "I knew that, of course. I'd seen it before."

"How do your fields look?"

"Muley got the corn planted before he and Ramón took and went to join Houston. Rain's got the field growed up in weeds pretty bad. It sure needs plowin'. And then, there's the garden to plant and all."

"That don't sound so bad, then. By your face, I thought it was goin' to be worse."

Buckalew glanced at Rebecca Provost and then back to Heather Winslow. "Ladies, I don't want to get you-all upset or nothin', but me and Muley, we found horsetracks. They was made in the mud, maybe a week or more ago, but tracks just the same. And they wasn't just wild mustangs wanderin' over the country. They had riders on them."

Provost's mouth curved downward. "Indians?"

"I expect."

"Could've been just a huntin' party, already long gone back west where they come from."

"Could've been."

"Might not see any more Indians around here for months . . . maybe not for a year."

"Might not. But if they *are* here, I damn sure want to see *them* before they see *me*."

Without being told, Heather sensed that they were near-
ing the Hernandez place. Ramón Hernandez kept drifting
farther and farther forward, till he was up even with Ocie
Quitman on the point. Rather than ride with him, Quitman
stopped his horse and waited for the wagons to catch up,
then he drifted out to Ramón's customary place on the
flank. Often Heather could see Ramón turn to look back
over his shoulder as if to ask why the wagons were moving
so slowly.

And finally she saw him take off his hat and wave it in a
wide circle over his head. The warm south breeze brought
the sound of lusty shouting. Beyond him she saw two
horses and made out the figures sitting on them. The riders
moved into a lope toward Ramón, and Ramón spurred into
a run. When they all reined up together, she could see
Ramón throw his arms around first one of the riders, then
the other.

She heard Dent Sessum grumble, "Hell of a lot of
guardin' he's doin' for us right now. A whole herd of Indians could ride in on us and he'd never even see them."

Heather felt compelled to speak. "He's found some of
his family. You can't blame him for that."

"I didn't know Mexicans had families. I figured they just
had litters, like dogs."

Heather wished she could have seen Joshua Buckalew
beat Dent Sessum instead of simply having to hear about it.

She could see that the two riders with Ramón were boys,
wearing plain homemade cotton shirts and trousers, with
floppy straw hats perched on their heads. Their feet were
bare except for simple leather *huaraches* which covered
little but the soles. Joshua Buckalew rode forward and em-
braced them. Muley Dodd jumped off of his horse, pulled
the boys down and whirled around and around with first
one of them, then the other. From fifty yards away, Heather
could hear his happy laugh.

As the wagons pulled up, Ramón put his hands on the two boys' shoulders and led them to the Provost wagon. "Mrs. Provost, Mr. Provost . . ." He glanced toward Heather. ". . . Mrs. Winslow, I want you all to meet my brothers. Demons, these two. But good demons."

The boys stared at the wagons and the people on them and made their *mucho gustos* with cautious grace and bubbling curiosity. Aaron climbed down and shook hands with them as if they were adults, and Heather could tell that the gesture had made him their friend for life. Aaron asked, "Ramón, did they give you a good report on the rest of your family?"

Ramón grinned. English failed him, and he replied in Spanish, which Heather understood imperfectly. "Everyone is well. My baby son is almost big enough to smoke tobacco, and I have not even seen him yet. Josh, I think I will ride on ahead."

"Go on, Ramón. We wouldn't have it no other way."

"Perhaps you would like to go in with me?"

Muley nodded his enthusiasm, but Josh waved him back. "No, Ramón, you have your reunion first. We'll be in with the wagons directly."

Muley was still eager. "Josh, I'd like to go with him."

"We'll need you here, Muley. With Ramón goin' on ahead, and all, we're a man short."

One of the boys spoke, "We'll tell María you are coming, Josh."

"You do that, Gregorio."

Heather frowned, for she had understood enough Spanish to catch that. She wondered who María was. It suddenly occurred to her that Josh had taken time this morning to shave his face clean. She hadn't given it much thought at the time except to note that he looked strongly handsome with the whiskers off.

Heather, she told herself, *it's none of your business. You've got no claim on the man. Maybe someone else has.*

But she wondered, nevertheless.

It was an hour before the wagons climbed the last hill and Heather looked down on the Hernandez *rancho*. At first glance she almost missed seeing the buildings. They were made of rock that blended with the color of the land around them. Their roofs were almost flat, so that the main house and the little buildings clustered close around it seemed to huddle just barely above the ground, and seemed to be almost a part of it. A scattering of gardens and green little fields lay on the slope and down in the shallow valley below the house. The fields had been freshly worked. They weren't weed-grown like those of the *Americano* settlers who had been forced to flee ahead of Santa Anna's army.

She heard Sessum grumble loudly to Ocie Quitman, "Looky yonder, will you? Everything neat as ever was. House standin', kids playin' in the yard. Couldn't even tell there was a war. A lot different than for all the white folks. All he's got to do is pick up things right where he left off. And him just a black-eyed Mexican. Kind of gorges you a little, don't it?"

Heather could not hear Quitman's reply, if he gave one. For a moment she found herself sharing a little of Sessum's resentment, until she realized that Ramón had fought for Texas, and Sessum hadn't fought for anything. He had been sitting on the Sabine, he and his partner McAfee, waiting for others to shed their blood and make the ground safe for him.

Aaron Provost spoke reprovingly, "Don't be envious, Sessum. Rejoice in another man's good fortune. Next time it may be yours."

"Damn it, Provost, there's that Mexican down yonder got him a good house and a bunch of fresh-plowed fields and it don't even make you a little bit mad. Don't *nothin'* ever provoke you?"

Aaron's eyes narrowed, and his voice went deliberately flat. "*You* provoke me sometimes, Sessum. It'd please me a right smart if you'd just tend your wagon and hold your silence."

Resentment flared in Sessum's face, but he said nothing more. Heather had an idea that one hard blow from the farmer's big fist could knock him off his wagon, and Sessum probably knew it. She had a devilish wish to see it happen but knew it was unlikely she ever would. Aaron Provost used his great strength for labor, not for strife. She had seen him grieve over that renegade boy he had shot. Provost would fight if he had to, but it would be with reluctance.

Josh and Muley rode down the hill a little ahead of the wagons. Muley broke loose and raced on, sliding his horse to a stop, jumping down and scooping up the smaller members of the Hernandez family one at a time, swinging them round and round. The youngsters then would run to Josh and throw their arms around him.

Heather could see Ramón and a tiny woman standing proudly by the door of the stone house, Ramón holding a red-blanketed bundle in his arms. Then she saw another woman who had moved out into the yard, behind the children but well in front of Ramón and his wife. This, Heather knew, would be the María whose name she had heard. María was watching Josh intently, her hands clasped in nervousness as she obviously fought a strong wish to run out and meet him halfway. Josh broke free of the youngsters finally, and he turned toward María. He stood there a moment, looking at her, then moved. She broke into a run and threw her arms around him.

The proper thing, Heather knew, would have been to look the other way and give them their moment of privacy. But she watched. She glanced at Ocie Quitman, finally, and she found he was watching, too. His eyes disapproved.

"You look troubled, Mister Quitman."

"Never did set good with me, seein' American men dally with these Mexican women. Always thought they ought to have more pride."

"Every man needs a woman sometime. There aren't enough American women to go around."

"Then a man ought to do without." Quitman looked at the ground. Face twisting, he swung down and dropped to one knee to examine a wide mark. "*Carreta* track. Been one of them big Mexican carts along here."

"I expect these people have one."

"This one passed not very long ago." Anger welled in his face, anger Heather could not understand. "Faustino!" he said bitterly.

"What is Faustino?"

"Never mind."

Ramón had all of his family line up. He introduced Aaron and Rebecca and Heather. He made no effort to introduce all the Provost children because he simply hadn't had a chance to get them all separated in his own mind. Last of all he named Ocie Quitman and Dent Sessum. Neither man did more than nod.

Heather said quietly to Quitman, "I know I have no right to criticize you . . ."

"No, you don't."

Muley's old hound Hickory made a fuss over him, then he and the Provosts' dogs warily circled, sizing each other up, testing one end and then the other.

Heather somehow thought at first that the Mexican children were sons and daughters of Ramón, but it was made clear to her they were his brothers and sisters. His father and mother had been taken by the fever before the war began. The only child he had of his own was the baby he proudly held in his arms, opening the blanket so everyone could see the tiny brown face, the dark eyes blinking defensively against the brightness of the sun. Ramón's wife Miranda stood beside him, smiling happily, her small hands tightly holding onto his arm as if she never intended ever again to let Ramón out of her grasp.

Heather had seen Mexicans before, but she had never been around them much. The few she saw were transient horse traders and the like, and the handful of resident Mexicans who lived in Austin's capital town of San Felipe. She could not remember that she had ever seen a family group like this one, at their own home and wholly at ease.

"They don't seem so different, do they, Mister Quitman? I mean, they remind me of when I was a girl, back home."

"They're different, Mrs. Winslow."

Ocie Quitman tied his horse to the wagon wheel and walked up to Ramón. Ramón opened the blanket a little to show his child, but Quitman didn't look down. He stared at Ramón. "How long since Faustino left here?"

Ramón's smile faded. "Forget Faustino. He is gone."

"I asked you, how long?"

"When I came. I saw him here, I told him go."

"You gave him stuff?"

"Food, blankets."

"I didn't want nobody helpin' them."

Ramón reverted to Spanish. "This is *my* place, Mister Quitman. *I* say who is helped here, and who is not. You are my guest, and *only* my guest."

Quitman turned toward his horse. "I can fix that. I don't have to stay here."

"Wait." Ramón pointed at the boy Patrick. "Your son has need of this place. Where would you take him?"

Quitman fought for control of his temper. He glanced toward Heather Winslow as if to ask her for help. She had none to give him. She said, "He's right, Mister Quitman."

Quitman stood with his back to Ramón. His fists clenched a moment, but slowly he gave in and turned. "All right, Hernandez. Long as Faustino has left for Mexico—long as he don't ever come back—I reckon that's the last I'll say of it. But I want you to understand one thing: you're not givin' me nothin'. Whatever you do for me or my boy, I'll pay for it. I'll pay you in work or in goods or in money, but I'll pay you. I'll not stand beholden."

Ramón nodded. "Then, I see no argument. We are agreed."

The first thing they had to do was to place the wagons, for they would have to continue to live out of them until the crops were planted and the cabins rebuilt. The teams were maneuvered so that the Provost wagon and Quitman's sat a few steps apart, not far from the stone house. Aaron Provost motioned for Dent Sessum to pull his into the same line, but Sessum hauled his team around and moved off down toward one of the sheds.

"No use us gettin' our stuff mixed up with each other," Sessum grunted. "Keep 'em apart, I say. Then there ain't no chance of one of us gettin' off with things that belong to somebody else and causin' hard feelin's." He spat, his gaze touching the house, then falling on some of the Hernandez youngsters. "Besides, the further I stay away from *them* people, the better I'll sleep of a night."

Provost made no argument. When Sessum was out of earshot, the big farmer sighed in relief, "I'll sleep a lot better knowin' he's that far away from *me*. He'd bust a gut if he thought somebody would get off with a tin cup or a piece of rope that belonged to him. I believe he's the greediest livin' thing I ever seen, outside of a hog pen."

Quitman turned toward Josh. "Where do you intend to camp?"

Josh grimaced. "I *had* figured on the shed. But with Sessum down there, Muley and me will have to find us some other place. That arbor, I expect."

Quitman frowned toward the door of the rock house, where María Hernandez had gone. "Kind of thought you might choose to camp with her."

Josh's voice sharpened. "You better get one thing straight, Quitman, and get it now. She's as honest as the best you ever met."

"If you say so." Quitman paused. "Mind if I camp with you?"

"Suit yourself. I'm surprised you'd want to."

"It's either you or Sessum. There's some things you do that I don't care for, but at least you're open about them."

Josh stared at him, still surprised. "I'd have to say the same for you, Quitman. Times, I'd like to take a club to you. But I always know where you stand."

As she had been doing on the trail each night, Heather Winslow shared camping chores with Rebecca Provost. Cooking together, washing the utensils together, they managed to make the load easier than if each tried to maintain a separate camp. The children helped unload what they would need out of the wagons. Aaron Provost dug a pit for the fire.

Heather noticed that the Hernandez youngsters gathered around, well out of the way, watching the Provost boys and girls and Ocie Quitman's son. The Provost children gawked back.

"Come on, young'uns," Mrs. Provost scolded, "we got work to be done." But it wasn't being done very efficiently. The oldest Provost boy had his eye on the oldest of the

Hernandez girls. Suddenly he leaped toward her and shouted, "Boo!" She jumped. The others giggled and laughed. Mrs. Provost shooed them all away. "Go on, all of you. You're no help here anyway. Go on out yonder and get yourselves acquainted."

Heather smiled. "You're not afraid they'll be contaminated?"

"You been listenin' to Ocie Quitman. A lot he knows . . ."

María Hernandez came out again and approached the two women hesitantly. "Pardon. Is there anything I can do to help?"

Mrs. Provost stretched, her hands pressing against her back. "I reckon we got it in order . . . as much order as we're goin' to have."

The Mexican girl said apologetically, "If the house was larger . . ."

Mrs. Provost shrugged, smiling. "Well, it ain't, and there's nothin' you can do about that, child. We'll have our own cabins in due time."

Heather Winslow studied María. She found her slight in build, not weighing much over a hundred pounds. Long black hair, carefully brushed and ribbon-tied at the back of her neck, framed a pretty oval face. It was the skin Heather noticed most—olive skin, clear and smooth, as if it had never known the harshness of the sun and the wind. Heather felt of her own face and knew it must be chapped and rough, for this had been a hard trip, and exposure had been extreme.

The girl's gaze moved to Heather, and Heather looked down, embarrassed to be caught staring. "I like your place here."

María Hernandez smiled. "It is home. Not pretty, like some places in Bexar. Have you ever been to Bexar?"

Heather shook her head. María went on, "It is very pretty in Bexar, or was before the trouble. Big stone houses by the river, tall churches, pretty gardens . . . You would like it."

"I like it here."

"I would be pleased to show you all of it."

"I'd like that. How about you, Rebecca?"

Mrs. Provost shook her head. "I'm a little tired, and anyway I got a meal to start. You young folks go ahead. I'll see it in due time, I expect."

María led Heather first to the house. Heather paused at the arbor in front of the door and looked at a couple of crude willow crates, which stood open and empty.

"For the roosters," María said. "The fighting roosters. My father, my older brothers, they all liked the fighting roosters. But the war came, and there was no more time."

"You mean people raise roosters just to fight?"

"They fight to the death, if you let them."

"How do they provoke them into it?"

"They do not have to. It is bred into the birds to hate and to fight. There does not have to be a reason. You put them together and they fight, that is all." Sadness touched her. "With people, it is the same. They do not need a reason. They just fight. They fight and they die, and they know not why they do it."

The house was as plain inside as outside, Heather found. The furniture was handmade from materials found close to home. The walls were mostly bare, coats hanging from pegs secured by the mortar between the stones. Heather's eye was caught by a huge hand-carved crucifix hanging in a corner, the figure of Christ meticulously done.

María said, "My father made that. He had the priest to bless it because we are so far from the church. We look at it, and we do not forget what is holy."

María started to lead her into another room but stopped. Heather caught a glimpse of Ramón and Miranda sitting on a bed, their hands clasped as they looked down on their sleeping baby. María smiled and whispered, "They have no need of us."

She led Heather outside and up the slope. Occasionally María would stop to point out one thing or another, and tell of some incident that had happened there.

Heather noticed a tall rock corral, quite close to the house. "A lot of work went into that. Why did it have to be built so strong? No animal is going to break out of it anyway."

"The Comanche might try to break in. When we know the Indians are close, we put the horses and mules in the rock corral. The gate is on the side by the house. When the Indians try to take the bars away and open it, we can stop them. Never have we lost an animal out of that corral."

"Do the Indians come often?"

"Not often. But when they come, they want horses."

The two women walked on up the slope and stopped finally at a small family cemetery where tall wooden markers stood stark against the blue sky. María crossed herself and pointed to the two tallest. "My mother and father. Next to them, a little brother who died of the fever at the same time."

On another cross Heather read the word. "Teresa."

"My sister," said María. "It was many years ago she died."

"The fever?"

"No, the Comanches. They found her on the road." She looked at the ground. "Do you know Joshua very well?"

"Not really. We came across him and your brother and Muley west of San Jacinto."

"Joshua was in love with Teresa. He wanted to marry her. That was a very long time ago."

Heather waited a little before she asked, "And now you want to marry *him?*" When María stared in surprise, Heather continued, "I saw the way you greeted him. It was plain to anyone with eyes that you were in love with him. Is he in love with you?"

María shook her head soberly. "I don't know. I don't think *he* knows. People all say I look like my sister. I know how he felt about *her*."

"How long have you been in love with him?"

"Since I was a little girl. He came here, he taught us English while we taught him Spanish."

"You speak it very well."

"Even as a girl, I wanted to please him. I studied hard. I learned English better than anyone here, even Ramón, and he knew it before, from Bexar. But I was foolish. I was only a little girl. Teresa was a woman."

"You're a woman now."

"Perhaps it is still not enough. Perhaps another woman will come along and he will love her instead of me."

Heather got an uneasy feeling María meant her. "I am not your rival, María."

María managed a thin smile. "I meant nothing. But I could not blame you if you wanted Josh. He has been wanted before."

"But no one ever got him."

"One day someone will. I hope it is me."

Down on the flat, Ocie Quitman rode alone, walking his horse, studying the fields, looking over the scattering of Hernandez cattle. María's eyes hardened with dislike as she watched him. "He is a strange one, your Mister Quitman."

"*My* Mister Quitman?"

"Well, Mister Quitman, anyway. Ramón told us he would be so. Before you came, a Mexican man and woman stopped here in an oxcart." They were in such a hurry they would not even let us cook for them. They were afraid Mister Quitman would come."

Heather's eyes widened, for now she started putting odd

bits of fact together, and she thought she could figure the rest of the story. She told María about Faustino and about Quitman's wife.

María's voice softened a little. "That, then, is why he dislikes us all."

"It's more than just dislike. He's a good man in many ways, but he's like one of your fighting roosters. He fights because it is in him to do it. Give him room, María. He's been hurt, badly. He may hurt a lot of others before he gets it burned out of his system."

VIII

IT TOOK ONLY A COUPLE OF DAYS TO CATCH UP WITH what work the men needed to do around the Hernandez place, for the women and the youngsters had stayed busy while Ramón was off to the war.

Dent Sessum bent his back but little. Most of the time he walked around admiring the fields or riding one of his horses bareback over the grassland. The longer he looked at it, the better he liked it. While Ramón squatted with Joshua Buckalew beside Josh's coffee bucket one evening, Sessum strode up and made a blunt offer. "I'll buy this place from you, Hernandez. I'll pay you in American cash money."

Surprised, Ramón shook his head. "It is not to be sold."

"Better take my offer, *hombre*. Next time I won't likely bid as much."

"Next time I don't sell, either. This is my home."

"Home is where a man lays his head down to sleep. You can sleep comfortable someplace else, with American money in your pockets."

"I will sleep here."

"You can take and buy you some more land."

"Why? I do not want other land. Why would I sell?"

Sessum squinted one eye. "Because you're a foreigner livin' in a white man's country, that's why. The war's over. Goin' to be a lot of new people move in here now, people from the States. They ain't goin' to take well to havin' Mexicans livin' in their midst. Like as not they'd up and run you off and you wouldn't get paid a thing. Better you take my offer and go hunt you a place where you're welcome."

Ramón pointed up the slope. "See that cemetery? My father is there, and my mother. Some others too. This is Hernandez land, for always. I have fought for it against Santa Anna."

"Them new people movin' in, they ain't goin' to know that, or care. All they'll see is that you're a Mexican. Believe me, Hernandez, they'll move you. Or they'll bury you up in that cemetery with the rest of your folks."

Ramón set his cup aside and stood up straight. His leg had healed enough that he no longer walked with a stick. "Do you make a threat?"

"A prediction. And you can mark it down as the gospel."

Joshua Buckalew pushed to his feet and stepped in front of Sessum. "You heard him tell you he don't want to sell. Now you leave him alone."

"Let him fight his own battles."

"He did, at San Jacinto. If you'd seen him there, you wouldn't be so damned anxious to stir up a fight with him now."

Glaring, Sessum turned and walked away resentfully.

Ramón went back to Spanish. "Josh, do you really believe he has the money he talks about?"

Josh nodded. "I expect. I've had a feelin' for a long time that he and McAfee had somethin' hidden in that wagon."

"Where do you think they got it?"

"Not much tellin'. They didn't earn it. And wherever it was, you can bet they left there in the middle of the night."

*   *   *

It was time for the men to go back and work their own farms
in Hopeful Valley, to break their weed-grown fields and
plant spring crops. They agreed to stay together for mutual
protection as well as for the speed and efficiency they would
gain by working as a team. They wanted to take Sessum's
wagon, for it would be sitting idle and unneeded here.

Josh was sure that by now Sessum had gone off somewhere in the dark and had buried his money, so the wagon
wasn't needed to store it. But Sessum argued that a wagon
was a tremendously valuable piece of equipment these
days, well-nigh impossible to replace. The trip would be a
hazard to it that he felt no obligation to suffer, especially
because he had no land yet and was, in his view, already
contributing more than his share by the labor he was per-
forming. That he worked at all was simply a demonstration
of the goodness of his heart, Sessum declared.

The upshot was that they took Ocie Quitman's wagon.
Heather Winslow said she could do without it. The men
loaded Ramón's wooden plows and tied his work oxen behind the wagon. They loaded axes and shovels, seed corn
and coffee. In the way of food, there was not much more
they could take. For the most part they would live off of the
land.

Muley watched the children at play, his eyes aglow.
"Josh, how about me stayin' here and kind of helpin' tend
to things? I could be a right smart of protection for the
womenfolk."

Josh smiled. He knew Muley wouldn't be very watchful
protection, for he would be playing games with the kids
every minute the women didn't have him busy on some job
or other. "Muley, we need you too bad ourselves. We've decided to leave Aaron's boy Daniel. He's not far from bein'
a man, and he can shoot as good as any of us, just about.

María can handle a rifle, and I expect Heather Winslow and
Rebecca Provost could too, if the need come. They'll be all
right, long as nobody strays far from the house."

Muley looked crestfallen. "Josh, I was helpin' them
Provost boys learn to talk Mexican. They're startin' to do
pretty good."

Josh's observation was that the boys had learned a lot
more from the Hernandez brood than from Muley. Muley's
Spanish was rudimentary and mostly wrong. "They won't
forget what you've taught them. When we get back, you
can take up where you left off."

Miranda Hernandez stood leaning against Ramón, and it
was hard to tell which one was holding the baby, for each
had an arm beneath it. Miranda wept silently, and Ramón
tenderly assured her it wouldn't be long before they would
be back.

Josh took María's hand. "If there's any sign of Indians,
we'll come back in a hurry. Meantime, you-all stick close
by. Don't let anybody get so far from the house that they
could be cut off."

"You are the ones to be careful, Josh." Pain was in her
eyes. "You will be a long way from help."

"We're takin' along our own. There's six of us."

Patrick Quitman was in his father's arms. "Now, son,"
Quitman was telling him, "you mind whatever Mrs.
Winslow tells you, and don't you be causin' her no grief.
I'll be back soon's I can."

"You goin' to take us home before long, Daddy?"

Quitman winced. "I don't know, son. We'll just have to
see."

"I sure do wish we could go home."

Quitman looked away, and Josh could read the thought
betrayed by the heavy furrows in the man's face. How
could they go to a home that no longer existed, that could
never exist again the way it had been?

Quitman warned, "You stay close to Mrs. Winslow. Don't you be runnin' off out of sight."

The boy hugged his father's neck. "All right, Daddy. *Vaya con Dios*."

Quitman stiffened. "Where'd you learn that?"

"From Gregorio." Patrick pointed to the largest of the Hernandez boys. "Gregorio knows everything."

The brown-skinned lad shrank back in consternation from the hostility in Quitman's eyes. Quitman said, "Mrs. Winslow!"

Heather Winslow stepped forward. Quitman handed Patrick to her and said sternly, "Whatever teachin' is to be done for my boy, I want you to do it, or me. There's too many things he needs to learn a lot more than talkin' Mexican."

María Hernandez spoke, her voice edged with quick anger. "Gregorio has meant no harm, Mister Quitman."

Quitman stared at her a long moment. "And let's see that no harm is done, Miss Hernandez. If I decide I want him to learn Mexican, or to learn anything else you people can teach him, I'll let you know."

He climbed up onto the wagon seat and flipped the reins, the team quickly settling into the traces.

María watched him with eyes as hard as black shale. "Josh, will you do something for me?"

"Whatever you want."

"Run over him with his wagon, first time you have the chance. Don't kill him dead. Just kill him a little bit."

Hopeful Valley had no town, no store, no central settlement. It was simply a name some optimistic settler had hung on the whole general area which included the Provost place and Winslow's and Quitman's and a dozen others. Someday perhaps there would be a town, or at least a tiny crossroads settlement, when enough people came. It was a long way short of that yet.

The men halted first at the Provost place, hobbling the horses, staking the oxen, unloading the plows in Aaron's weedy field. The farmer took off his floppy hat and ran his huge hands through his graying hair, shaking his head as he gazed across the ragged, overgrown rows. "There's a heap of back strain ahead of us if we're to get any corn and cotton out of that mess this year."

Dent Sessum grunted. "Well, I'll stand guard and keep the Indians off of the rest of you, but I'll be damned if I see why I ought to break my back tryin' to make the other man a crop."

Josh flung a hard glance at him. At times, he wished it had been Sessum instead of his unlucky partner McAfee who had died under that Redlander's knife. "Don't you fret, Aaron. With all those kids you got, we have to see that you make a crop. Else it'll be up to the rest of us to feed you."

Aaron grinned. He called, "Hey, Muley, want to help me dig up a couple of graves?"

Muley looked stunned. "Well, Aaron, I was fixin' to help Ramón skin out this here deer we shot. We'll be needin' some supper."

"The deer can wait. Grab you a shovel, Muley."

Muley looked anxiously to Josh, but Josh jerked his thumb after Aaron in silent command. Muley put away his skinning knife, picked up a shovel and went trailing with no enthusiasm. Josh winked at Ramón and followed the farmer.

Provost stopped where three crosses stood over a set of mounds beneath a huge old live oak tree. He wrapped his muscular arms around one of the crosses and pulled it up, dropping it to one side. Muley's gaze followed the cross, then cut back to Aaron, scandalized as the farmer said, "All right now, let's get to diggin'."

"Aaron!"

Grinning, the farmer rammed his shovel into the mud. "Go ahead, Muley. Anything that's down there ain't alive."

"No, sir, I wouldn't hardly think so."

Muley made a few perfunctory jabs with the shovel, his spirit not in it. Aaron had to do most of the digging. Presently his blade struck something. The sharp sound brought Muley's eyes wide open. Aaron knelt and cleared the wet earth from around a plowhandle. "Help me pull it up, Muley." Muley didn't move. Aaron finally had to tell him, "It's not nothin' like you think it is. Help me, Muley."

"It ain't nothin' dead?"

"No, Muley. I was funnin' you."

Muley stepped into the hole and helped tug. Josh reached down and took hold. They brought up a muddy plow.

Aaron said, "We buried everything we couldn't haul with us on the Scrape. We put the crosses up to fool the Mexicans."

Muley wiped his face. "Mexicans wasn't all you fooled, Aaron. That was a real funny joke." But he wasn't laughing.

In a little while they had dug up a considerable variety of tools from the first two "graves." Aaron said, "We'd best smooth these holes over and leave the third one like it is. Mostly it's got Rebecca's kitchen things in it. They'll be safer right where they're at."

The labor was hard and steady, for the weeds were rank and clung stubbornly to life. But the soil had dried enough on top that it worked without balling on the plows. The men used all the equipment they had, and all the animals, methodically turning up the fresh brown earth in rows straight as an arrow. They finished Aaron's fields, planting the corn and putting in the garden. Next they moved to the widow Winslow's place and did the same. That done, they went on to Ocie Quitman's.

Muley Dodd had a strong back, and work held no terror for him. But his was not a nature that could go indefinitely on hard labor without some relief. The third day at Quitman's, Josh noticed Muley's plow leaned idle in the row, the horse standing switching flies. Josh could see the rust color of Muley's holey shirt moving through the timber. Presently Muley came to the field in a trot, his face aglow with excitement.

"I seen some wild bees, Josh. I could find us some honey if you'd give me leave."

Josh looked across the field, surveying the large amount of work still to be done. But he knew Muley wouldn't be much help when his thoughts turned to bee-hunting. Muley's mind had a hard time keeping track of more than one thing at a time.

"I reckon it'd be all right if you had somebody to go with you for protection. Try Dent Sessum. He ain't been much help to us anyway." It would be a relief to get Sessum out of sight anyway. An idle man is always an irritant to the one who has to work. Besides, Josh knew the others were getting as tired of their straight venison diet as he was. They were low on coffee and cornmeal and hadn't had any sugar at all.

For days now, Muley had been watching for bees. He had already made his preparations, stripping a deerhide off without slitting it down the belly. He had turned it wrong-side out, sewed up the bullethole and tied off the legs with buckskin strings. Then he had blown it up tight and let it dry in the sun. Now it was a tight case, big enough to hold all the honey a strong man could carry.

Muley slung the empty skin case over his shoulder. He carried an ax in one hand and a rifle in the other. Dent Sessum frowned, dubious about the whole adventure. He eased up to Josh and asked suspiciously, "You sure you ain't just sendin' me off on a fool's errand? Muley ain't smart enough to know a bee from a hummin' bird."

"Everybody's got his own talent. Bee-huntin' is Muley's."

Sessum snorted. "I'll wager he can't even find a wasp's nest. Tell you what, Buckalew: ever bit of honey he gits, I'll tote in on my own back."

Josh said to Muley, "You remember that now. He made you a promise." Muley grinned in excitement. Josh pointed a finger at him. "Don't you get so wrought up over your bees that you forget to watch out for Indian sign. You keep a sharp eye open, Muley."

"I will, Josh. You comin', Mister Sessum?"

When they were gone out of sight, Josh went back to his plow. They put in a long day of it and had the biggest part of the field turned by sundown. Josh stood stretching, both hands on his hips, and searched the landscape futilely for a sign of Muley and Sessum.

Aaron Provost climbed up from the creek where he had been washing the dirt and sweat from his face and hands. "You don't reckon somethin' went with them?"

Josh shook his head. "We'd of heard shootin'. Once Muley gets on a bee trail, he just don't know when to quit." He turned and watched Ramón Hernandez limp in from the field, walking his oxen.

Aaron followed Josh's gaze. "That leg's still gimpy."

"Mornin's, it looks like Ramón has healed up. You don't see much of a limp. Evenin's, time he's put in a hard day, it comes back."

"He's workin' too hard. You better talk to him, Josh."

"That's always been Ramón's nature. When he works, he works hard. When he plays, he plays like it's for the last time."

"You better talk to him anyway." Aaron turned his attention to Josh. "By the bye, how's your arm?"

Josh blinked, and he rubbed the place where the saber had cut. He couldn't feel anything. In fact, he hadn't even thought about it. "I'd forgotten anything happened."

Ocie Quitman brought in the team he had been working to a heavy plow. He walked them over the steep creek bank, a way downstream from where Ramón was watering the oxen.

Aaron frowned. "Bank's almost flat where Ramón is. Plenty of room for all of them. Ocie don't have to go down the steep place."

"Just can't bring himself to get that close to Ramón."

"Think he'll ever come around?"

"He's been burned awful deep."

"You notice the way he's acted since we been here on his farm? Hasn't said three words in three days."

Josh nodded. "He told me he didn't think he could ever live here again. Too many ghosts. It'll be a good thing for him when we finish up and get off of this place."

Aaron kindled a campfire out of the banked coals. "It'll be better when he gets married again and has a soft, warm woman to smooth the rough edges off of him. I got an idea a woman like Heather Winslow could help make a man forget that one that died."

"He ain't said he figures to marry her. And I don't recall she's said anything about it, either."

"It'll happen. They need each other too bad." Aaron smiled tolerantly. "Besides, Rebecca has made up her mind to it. When that wife of mine decides a thing is goin' to be, you better take it for gospel."

Ramón turned the oxen loose to graze on the lush green grass along the creek. At dark the men would have to gather all the stock and pen them in a brush corral thrown together for protection against befeathered horse thieves.

Finishing, Ramón picked up the empty water bucket. Aaron took it from him. "You set yourself down and rest. That leg must be givin' you fits. I'll tote the water."

"Leg's all right," Ramón protested. But he didn't argue much, so Josh took it that the leg was aching.

Slicing venison from a deer leg hanging suspended below a live oak branch, Josh said, "You got to go a little easier, Ramón. That leg is liable to cripple on you, permanent."

"The sooner we get all the fields plowed out and planted, the sooner I get home to Miranda and the baby."

"You don't want to go home on a bad leg. Tomorrow we'll find you somethin' easier to do. You won't be lookin' them oxen in the rear."

"I am not Dent Sessum."

"You're lame. He's just lazy. It's a religion with him."

Ramón sat up straight and pointed. "Then he is losing his religion."

Turning, Josh began to laugh. Muley Dodd came striding out of the timber, rifle in one hand, ax in the other. Behind him—way behind—Sessum struggled along, his back bent under the heavy load of the bulging deerskin.

Muley shouted long before he reached the camp. "Told you, Josh. Told you I could course me some bees. You ought to see what I found."

Josh waited until Muley came up to him. "I *do* see. If you'd of found any more, you'd of broken Sessum's back."

"That'd be a good idea," Aaron grumbled.

Muley glanced over his shoulder, then back to Josh. His voice dropped almost to a whisper. "Josh, I think I ought to tell you somethin'. That Mister Sessum, he ain't a nice feller."

Josh tried to act surprised. "What did he do?"

"He wanted to go back on his promise. He kept settin' the

honey down and swearin' he wouldn't carry it another step. But a promise is a promise, ain't it, Josh? You always told me if I promised to do somethin' I got to do it. I told him that, and he wouldn't listen." Muley's voice reflected his disapproval. "But I foxed him, Josh. I told him I was fixin' to run off and leave him out in them woods all by hisself. He'd holler a little bit and then pick up the honey again. He'd carry it a ways, and then it was all to do over. He ain't very nice."

Dent Sessum struggled into camp and let the honey skin down. His face and hands were swollen, for the bees hadn't taken the robbery without a fight. Muley showed not a wound. This one thing, at least, he knew how to do.

Aaron Provost ran his finger through some honey that had seeped out around the bullethole. "First honey I've tasted since I don't remember when. You fellers'll have to do this some more."

Sessum groaned. "Like hell. I'd rather follow a mule backwards and forwards over that field than follow this halfwit across all creation."

Angering, Josh said, "Tomorrow you remember you said that, because that's just what you're goin' to do."

Sessum flared. "I still ain't got no land of my own. I don't see as I need to do anything I don't want to."

Ocie Quitman had walked up, shoulders slumped in weariness, eyes bleak from the strain of being on this place that held so many memories. Somehow Sessum's complaint sparked a sudden blaze of anger. Quitman grabbed Sessum's collar and jerked. "You'd sure as hell better want to, or you'll sack your plunder and move out of here. Tomorrow you're goin' to sweat, Sessum, or I'm goin' to see you leave."

Sessum swallowed. He trembled a little after Quitman turned loose of his collar. He finally collected enough strength to declare, "All right, I been abused enough. First thing in the mornin' I'll head up to the Mexican's place and get my wagon and clear out. I got nothin' at stake with you people. You can just get along without me."

Quitman strode angrily away, past the other men. He grabbed the ax and began chopping firewood with a fury that couldn't have been caused by Sessum alone. Sessum had merely set off the fuse. Aaron rubbed his whiskery chin and stared through narrowed eyes. "He's got a terrible anger buildin' in him, Josh. He's takin' out a little of it on that ax. But it's goin' to be dangerous for the man that ever causes him to let all that steam out at once. You better keep Ramón clear of him."

Next morning, true to his word, Sessum saddled after a hasty breakfast and took off, riding north. In a way Josh hated to see him go. Little as Sessum had done, at least he had been an extra gun in case trouble came.

Before noon Sessum came riding back. Quietly he unsaddled and hobbled his horse. He carried his saddle and blanket and bridle up close to the camp fire and dropped them. He stared into the blaze a few moments before he could bring himself to look anybody in the eye. Finally he said in a subdued voice, "A man'd be a fool to ride across that country by hisself. It ain't nothin' you can see, but I swear you can almost smell the paint and feathers in every thicket. Bad as I hate it, I reckon we need each other."

Josh and Muley's corn crop was already well underway because Muley had planted it before he left with Ramón to join Sam Houston. It was overgrown now in weeds, so the main task was to hoe it without uprooting the corn. They turned in on the job with hands and hoes.

A day's work done, they huddled around the campfire, frying venison. Aaron pointed his square chin at Josh's field. "Josh, you're goin' to have you a corn crop laid by while the rest of us is still just thinkin' about it."

"There'll be enough here to feed everybody till the harvest comes in for the rest of you."

"Thanks, Josh. We knowed you'd feel that way. We'll pay you back when the time comes." His gaze drifted northward. "Sure am missin' Rebecca and the young'uns. Wisht we had our cabin up so we could all be closer home."

Josh said, "I been studyin' how'd be the best way to handle it, and whose cabin we ought to put up first. Way I see it, we ought to go ahead and build yours, Aaron, soon's we get my fields weeded."

Sessum spoke up, though it wasn't any of his business whose house was built first. "Why his? Why not somebody else's?"

"First place, Aaron's about as well located as anybody . . . in the center of things, I mean. Second place, he's got far and away the biggest family. Way I see it, we build Aaron's first. We build it big enough to take care of the extra folks awhile. By extra folks I mean Mrs. Winslow, and Quitman and his boy. And you too, Sessum, till you find a place for yourself. Muley and me, our place is closer to Ramón's than it is to Hopeful Valley. Anyway, we can camp on the creek bank all summer if we have to. We don't have to have a roof before winter." He glanced at Quitman. "How does that sound to you?"

Quitman nodded. "Makes sense."

"Way I see it," Aaron put in, "Mrs. Winslow is a special kind of case. Even if we was to go and build her a cabin, she couldn't hardly live there by herself. And she sure couldn't live with you, Ocie, 'less the minister come around first. It wouldn't look right. So what I'd figured was that Rebecca and me would make a place for her at our house. She can read and write good, so I figured she could teach all them young'uns of ours. Your boy too, Ocie. In return for her teachin', we'd give her a roof and take care of her till you two figure a proper time has passed and you marry each other."

Quitman poked a fresh chunk of wood into the fire. "You're takin' a right smart for granted, Aaron. Mrs. Winslow and me, we haven't talked about the idea of marriage."

"You will," Aaron said confidently. "Nature will get to you bye and bye. A man needs a woman, even if he *ain't* got a boy that's without a mother. And a woman needs a man, especially if she's ever had one and got used to it. You'll both get to thinkin' about it as cold weather comes on. Them two farms would make one nice big place, once you join them together."

Quitman's eyes narrowed. "I'm not ready to think about things like that."

Aaron nodded. "I know, so your friends have got to do that thinkin' for you, and have things prepared when you do get ready."

"Aaron, you meddle like an old woman."

"One of life's little pleasures. Costs nothin' and does a heap of good in the world."

After supper they lay on their blankets in the grass beside the log corral Josh and Muley and Thomas Buckalew had built years ago. Josh stared into the darkening sky, wishing the work were done, wishing he could get back and see María again. He thought of her much these long days, and these nights. He thought of the shining laughter in her dark eyes, like the laughter he remembered in the eyes of Teresa so awfully long ago. Sometimes, it was hard to be sure which sister he thought of, for they had looked alike, these two.

Time had slowly healed the pain of Teresa's death. He had almost forgotten what she looked like, though the emptiness remained. Then one day he had gazed into the eyes of María and had seen Teresa there. The love he had once felt for Teresa had been born again, this time for María. The loneliness of the years between had left him in the light of María's smile.

Muley's voice came in a shout. "Josh! There's somebody out yonder horseback. Josh!"

Josh was on his feet instantly, grabbing for his rifle. The men around him scrambled for their guns. The fire had burned down to coals, but everyone hurried to get away from it. If these were Indians, they would be looking for targets by the red glow.

A long call came from the edge of the timber. "Hello-o-o! Hello the house!"

Josh relaxed a little. It wasn't Indians. It occurred to him that was a hell of a poor choice for a call, because there was no house unless you counted the charred heap of rubble. He thought he detected something familiar about the voice. He shouted. "Who's out there?"

"Josh! Is that you, Joshua Buckalew?"

Josh gritted, "Damn!", for he knew the voice now. He shouted back, "Come on in. It's all right."

Ocie Quitman lowered his rifle. "I take it this is some friend of yours?"

"Don't know as I'd want to call him a friend. Acquaintance is more like it. He neighbors me to the north. Name is Alfred Noonan. He's a lazy old hound dog of a man who'd talk the bark off of a tree. Quarrelsome, got a tendency to be a little mean. Don't never lend him nothin'."

Alfred Noonan rode in the lead, his gray beard streaming a little in the breeze. A second man rode half a length behind him, and Josh couldn't see him well in the poor light.

"Josh, boy!" Old Noonan's gravelly voice rubbed like splintery wood. "I'd of swore you was killed in the big war.

Didn't have no idea you'd come back till we seen your smoke awhile ago."

"Who's with you, Noonan?"

"See for yourself, Josh. It's Jacob Phipps, come back from the dead. Him that the Mexicans thought they'd killed way down below the Nueces. He come back, Josh, same as you did." Noonan quickly glanced over the faces. "I don't see Thomas. Was he . . ."

"He was killed."

Noonan nodded. "I'd of swore he was. Thought you was too. Thought everybody was but me. Then I come up on Jacob Phipps, and now you. The Lord's been bountiful in His mercy."

Jacob Phipps rode forward. He was thinner than Josh remembered him, and gray before his time, for Phipps was a young man yet, not even thirty. What Josh noticed most was the stiff left arm, hanging useless at Phipps' side. "Get down, Jacob. You had any supper?"

Phipps swung down and stretched out his right hand uncertainly. Josh gripped it. Phipps said, "I wasn't sure how you'd take it, me comin' here. We didn't always get along, me and you."

That was true, for Jacob Phipps and his brother Ezekiel, together with Noonan, had often been a thorn in Josh's side. From what Josh had heard, Ezekiel lay somewhere down near the Rio Grande, his head blown off by Mexican cavalry who had ambushed a foolhardy Texan patrol as Santa Anna's column started its march toward the Alamo.

Josh said, "Good to see you alive, Jacob. As for the rest, forget it. The past is gone." He pointed to the ruins of his cabin. "The future is all we got."

Phipps nodded sadly. "That's the truth if ever was. They didn't leave us nothin' but prospects. You say you got somethin' to eat?"

Josh introduced them around, though he found they'd

met Aaron before, and there seemed a slight recognition of
Ocie Quitman. They came finally to Ramón. Phipps shook
hands with him, but Noonan stepped back, disapproving.
"You mean, Josh, after all that's happened, you're still runnin' with *that* tribe?"

Regretfully Josh said, "I hoped the war would've changed
you, Noonan."

"I hoped it'd change *you*. Your brother dead, and still
you make friends with the likes of this?"

"Ramón fought on *our* side."

Noonan shrugged. "Knowed us Texans was bound to
win, that's why. They're a shifty lot, them people. Always
watch whichaway the wind blows, and they go with it. He
knowed we'd come out on top of old Santy Anna."

Josh's voice took on a barb. "Last time I seen you,
Noonan, *you* didn't think so. You had your tail between
your legs, runnin' for the Sabine River just as hard as you
could go."

Noonan's reddish face got even redder, but he made no
direct reply. "You watch. Hernandez and his kind will turn
against us first time they see a chance. You can't trust them
a minute."

Ramón limped away, angry but carrying it with him
rather than be the cause of trouble. Dent Sessum took old
Noonan by the arm. "You look hungry, friend. Come on
and we'll see what we can stir up for you. You sound like a
man after my own heart."

Josh glanced at Jacob Phipps. "How about you, Jacob?
Noonan speakin' for you, too?"

Phipps shook his head. "Me, I had all the fightin' I ever
want. I'm ready to be friends with everybody, white,
brown, black or green. I stick with Noonan because I need
him." He touched his dead arm. "But he don't do my
talkin' for me, not anymore."

IX

Mᴀʀíᴀ Hᴇʀɴᴀɴᴅᴇᴢ sᴛᴏᴘᴘᴇᴅ ɪɴ ᴛʜᴇ ᴇᴅɢᴇ ᴏғ ᴛʜᴇ garden and leaned on her hoe, gazing across the fields at the children, scattered up and down the long rows with hoes or bare hands, cutting or pulling the upstart young weeds that still tried to take hold among the corn-stalks and the cotton. They had gone farther from the house than María had told them to. Squinting, she could see the oldest Provost boy Daniel, way down at the far end of the field, near his tied horse. Daniel held a rifle and was supposed to be keeping watch. But María noted that he was bending a lot, evidently pulling weeds with the rest of them.

"They have gone too far, Heather," María said. "We must speak to them about that."

Heather Winslow was on her knees, digging up onions. She pushed her bonnet back away from her eyes. "Children don't always listen. Do you see Patrick?"

"Way out yonder by Daniel."

"He's always tagging after one of the older boys, either Daniel or Gregorio. He's gotten awfully attached to that young brother of yours."

"I know. And your Mister Quitman will not like it."

Mrs. Winslow reddened. "I wish you wouldn't call him *my* Mister Quitman."

"Mrs. Provost talks as if it is all settled."

"It isn't. I wish people would stop trying to push us into something I'm not sure either one of us wants."

"He is not a bad man to look upon. I cannot say I like his temper."

"He is bitter. He suffered a terrible loss."

"So did you. You do not seem bitter."

"Some people accept things, and others don't. I've accepted what happened to Jim. It was part of the war. In a way I guess it was to be expected. But what happened to Mister Quitman's wife was not to be expected. It was too cruel even for war."

"He seems a hard man, but he is gentle with you, Mrs. Winslow. That means something, yes?"

"I think he must always have been gentle with *her*."

María frowned. "And so maybe you only remind him of her."

"Maybe."

María's eyes pinched. "I hope it is not so. One should be loved for oneself, not because one reminds a man of someone else. That would be a long and empty road, I think."

The corner of her eye caught a sudden flurry of movement, and she turned half around, staring out across the field. She saw the Provost boy running, leading the horse. The boy Patrick was racing alongside him. Near them, some of the girls had dropped their sticks and hoes and were running toward young Provost. Daniel lifted them up and put them on the horse one at a time until four girls were astride. María saw him wave his hat and start the horse running toward the house. Then Daniel was running again, keeping his pace slow enough that Patrick could stay up.

Daniel shouted, though María could make out nothing he said. Nearer the house, the other children had caught the

importance of the sudden movement and seemed to be
hearing what Daniel was shouting at them. They dropped
everything and started to run.

Heather Winslow's face went pale. "María, what is it?"
But she must already have known.

María was already running. "There is a rifle in the
house. Come on!" She grabbed the rifle, a powderhorn and
a pouch of shot. She was out of the house again in seconds.
She paused only long enough to prime the weapon. Then
she was running for the field, racing toward the children.
Heather hurried just behind her.

The four girls on the horse came galloping past the other
running children. María threw her hands in the air as the
horse approached her. The biggest girl reined to a stop, and
María started helping the girls to the ground. "Run!" she
shouted. "Run for the house!" Then she motioned for
Heather. "Up! I'll give you a foot-lift."

Heather's long skirts got in her way, but she swung up,
sliding the skirts far up her legs. She reached down and
caught María's hand, helping María swing up too. María's
bare heels thumped against the horse's ribs as she reined it
around. The horse reluctantly went into a lope again. It had
caught the excitement and wanted only to go to the house.
María kept her heels drumming till she came up even with
the second group of running children. She shouted, "Down,
Heather. Take the rifle and get these children to the house.
I'll go for the boys."

Heather pointed to a line of horsemen on the hill, riding
down toward the field. "No, María, you can't. Look yonder."

"I think I can beat them to the boys."

Heather slid to the ground, falling to hands and knees
and pushing herself up immediately. She reached for the rifle and horn and pouch. María said breathlessly, "You can
reach the house before them, but keep the children moving
fast. Use the gun if you have to."

María moved away from Heather in a lope, her heels drumming again. Heather began pushing the children. "Hurry. Run, girls. Boys, rush it up. You've got to run." For herself, she was running backward much of the time, watching María.

The horse galloped through the fresh green corn, trampling the stalks, almost losing his footing in the soft plowed ground. María was shouting first at the horse, then at the boys. "Run, run!"

The riders were coming down off of the hill, yipping and shouting. María's blood ran like ice, and her scalp prickled. Comanches, smelling blood. It mattered not to them whether they killed men or women or children, or whether they were American or Mexican.

I'm not going to get there in time. The terrible thought ran through her mind, and scalding tears burned her eyes. Neither boy was hers, or even of her blood, but the thought of seeing them slain like helpless deer brought an anguished "No!" from her tight throat. She drummed her heels harder. Another thought came. What if they did not kill the boys? What if they took them? The Comanches did that sometimes with children. She had known of many cases. The boys, if they survived the first hard days and weeks, might be treated first as slaves and later taken into the tribe. The girls might also be enslaved, and when they were old enough, taken for wife.

Better they die, she thought. *But better still if I reach them first. Then at least they'll have a chance.*

María held no illusions about what the Indians would do if they caught *her*. Years ago, they had caught her sister Teresa.

The boys were only fifty yards from her now . . . forty . . . thirty. She dared not look for the Indians, but some terrible curiosity forced her to do it anyway. She saw that they were not coming straight at her now. They were angling off.

The ravine. She remembered the ravine which cut across above the field. It was too deep, too steep. They were having to go around it. She remembered the many times Ramón had cursed that ravine for stealing runoff water the field needed, and now she thanked God for it.

She stopped the horse and reached down for Patrick's arm. The Provost boy gave the lad a boost. Then, almost in the same motion, Daniel swung up too, the rifle still unfired but ready.

Three on one horse, and the Indians all riding single. That made for a desperate risk, but there was no way to ease it, for which boy would she leave? She shouted, "Hold me, Patrick," and put her heels to work again. They quartered across the field, trying to get out of the plowed soil and onto the solid ground. She glanced back once, just long enough to see the Indians coming around the head of the ravine. They were close enough that she could hear their shouts, even over the hoofs and the little boy's sobs.

Ahead, Heather Winslow was almost out of the field with the other children. There remained a run of fifty yards to the house. They could make it. Heather turned and faced back across the field, the rifle coming up to her shoulder. María saw the fire and the smoke and saw Heather drop the rifle butt to the ground, preparing to ram down another load.

"She's trying to help us," María told the boys.

Daniel Provost's voice was frightened. "She can't hit them at that distance."

"She will worry them," María said.

Daniel looked back and gasped. "There's one of them way out in the lead. He's goin' to catch us, María."

She saw an arrow go by like the flash of a light, suddenly gone. "Can you shoot him?"

He tried to aim the rifle. "Not with us goin' thisaway."

"Then be ready. I'll stop. Shoot him."

She reined to a quick halt. The rifle boomed. Daniel shouted, "He's down. I got the horse."

María put the plowhorse back into a run. Ahead of her, Heather Winslow fired again and began to retreat, moving backward, watching, reloading as she moved. María shouted, "To the house, Heather. Run!"

Heather fired once more, then turned and ran. María allowed herself another glance over her shoulder. The Indians were coming, but now María was certain she would beat them to the house. She slid to a stop as Heather reached the arbor. Rebecca Provost held the door open. "You-all come a-runnin'! Come a'runnin', I say!"

María shoved both boys off of the horse. Patrick sprawled, sobbing. Heather grabbed him into her arms. María turned the horse into the stone corral and took time to shut the gate. Rebecca Provost shouted desperately at her, and at her oldest son. But Daniel stood his ground at the arbor, rifle to his shoulder, protecting María. She sprinted for the house. The Provost boy walked backward, keeping the rifle ready. The dogs scurried through the door ahead of María. The boy turned and ran. Rebecca Provost slammed the door shut behind them and dropped the heavy bar.

María's lungs ached. She had held her breath much of the time, taking it in gasps. She found herself trembling now, tears starting to flow. She looked fearfully around the room, counting. "The children . . ."

Rebecca Provost hugged Heather, then María. "They're all here, praise God. Hadn't been for you two girls, we'd of lost them all." The older woman let her tears stream without any effort to blink them away. María broke free, still struggling for breath. "Heather . . . you have the rifle . . . Will you use it . . . or you want me to?"

Hands shaking, Heather extended the rifle to arm's length. "If you can shoot straight, you'd better do it."

Miranda Hernandez sat on the floor, cradling her baby to her bosom and praying softly to her saint. Rebecca and Heather got all the whimpering children to lie flat around Miranda. María went to a shuttered window. Daniel Provost was at another, peering intently through the port.

Rebecca said, "Heather, you got more learnin' than me. Miranda's prayin' in her language. You pray in English. The good Lord ought to understand *one* of you."

Heather asked, "What're *you* going to do?"

Rebecca had brought the chopping ax in from the wood-pile during the excitement. Now she picked it up. "I'm goin' to be holdin' this, just in case."

Hoofs pounded in the yard outside. An Indian made for the corral where María had penned the horse. Daniel's rifle roared. The bullet whined angrily off of the rock fence. "Didn't hit him," the boy shouted, "but he sure turned back." He began reloading.

An Indian galloped straight toward the house, lance poised. He hurled it, and the heavy wooden door trembled. María fired. The rider shrieked and flopped back, almost losing his leg-hold on the gotch-eared pony. As he whirled away, María glimpsed a blood-splotch on his side. She had creased his ribs, if she hadn't shattered them.

She took count of the Indians now. Six. Horse-stealing party, likely, but a party out for horses would not pass up any easy opportunity to bleed their enemies.

She saw two Indians riding one horse. One of them must have been the warrior Daniel had set afoot. For all practical purposes, then, they had put two Indians out of any real chance at action.

"Watch the corral!" she said to Daniel. "They'll try again for the horse. They have a man afoot."

One Indian got as far as the gate. His pony went down threshing, a slug in its belly. The Indian scuttled away.

The Comanches pulled back, shouting in anger. María knew none of the words, but the message was clear. Six men had only four horses between them now, and all the enemy were forted up in a strong rock house. Under normal circumstances the Indians would have left, for the Comanche was not one to throw his life away in a mad gamble. He killed when the odds were in his favor, and he melted with the whistling wind when the risk became too great. He was never ashamed to retreat, for retreat to him was not surrender. It was merely a realistic acceptance of a bad situation. He always intended to come back another time, when perhaps the spirits were smiling upon him.

For these men, retreat must be coming a little harder. They had seen nothing here but women and children. They probably were figuring accurately that if there had been any men here they would have come out to protect their families. It would be a galling thing for a Comanche warrior to go into camp and admit he had been set afoot and chased away by a few women and children.

"Be ready," said María. "I think they will try again."

She wished for more rifles. The Indians seemed to have none at all. They had used nothing but arrows and the lance, which she felt sure must still be stuck in the heavy door. "Can you see them, Daniel?"

"No. They're off to one side someplace. I can't see them through the porthole."

María moved across the room to watch the back of the house. She could see them out there milling around, uncertain, four men on horses, one standing, one sitting hunched on the ground, holding his side.

In the tightly closed room the dogs were barking and some of the children were whimpering. Their ears all rang from the roar of the rifles. Smoke hung thick and acrid. The children who weren't crying were coughing, choking on the smoke.

María saw one Indian come running, afoot. The horse-men gave him a few seconds, then came in a gallop, yip-ping and shouting.

"Two are coming your way, Daniel."

Two riders rushed toward the back of the house, but at such an oblique angle María could not take aim through the port. She held her fire and waited. An arrow thumped into the wooden shutters. Another struck the wood at the edge of the port and came flying in, its force blunted. It hit the rifle, glancing off. María's heart leaped with fright, but she forced herself to glance through the port. She saw the Indian afoot hurl his body against the shutters. The bar bulged and cracked. Almost in panic, María shoved the muzzle through the port and fired.

She realized instantly that had been a mistake, for now she had to take time to reload. The Indian threw his shoulder against the shutters again. The bar splintered, and the shutters swung open. For a second the Comanche paused there, blinking against the darkness of the interior while María fought to reload.

Mrs. Provost shouted, "You bloody heathen!" She ran at the Indian, the ax poised over her shoulder. The Indian tried to swing his bow into position to loose an arrow at her, but he was off balance. Just as the ax swung, he threw himself backward, out of the window. The blade split the bow and sank deep into the wooden sash. Mrs. Provost yanked it free, shouting in fury: "Hyahh-h-h, you red hea-then! Git! Git, I say!"

Weaponless now, he got. One of the dogs jumped through the window and raced after him, teeth bared.

María had her rifle reloaded. She stood back away from the window a little, trying not to make a target but ready to shoot when she had to.

Across the room, Daniel's rifle roared. "I got another horse!"

The Indians didn't try again. There were still six of them, and only three horses now. Even as it was, they would all have to ride double. They couldn't afford to lose another horse.

From her vantage point behind the broken shutters, María watched the Indians gather out of range. For a long time they milled, hands gesturing in argument. But cool heads prevailed, and presently the six Comanches melted away.

It was a long time before anyone ventured to open the door. When at last they worked up the nerve, Rebecca Provost slid the bar away, and Daniel pushed the door open. The lance bumped against a post supporting the arbor, and it clattered to the ground. Daniel moved out first, rifle poised. María and Heather went next, and finally Rebecca and Miranda.

Daniel picked up the lance, touching his thumb experimentally to the sharp metal point. "Filed out of a barrel hoop." He stepped into the yard. There two Indian horses lay, one dead, one slowly dying. Out at the field's edge lay another. There was no powder or lead to be wasted. He moved to the dying horse, slipped his Bowie knife from its sheath and cut the animal's throat. Walking back to the arbor, he said, "We didn't kill any Indians, looks like, but we sure played hell with their horses." He glanced at his mother, and his face reddened. "Mama, I hadn't ought to've said that."

Rebecca Provost threw her arms around him. "A boy ain't supposed to, but today you're a man. And a man can say anything he damn pleases."

X

AARON PROVOST BACKED OFF AND TOOK A LONG LOOK at the big new double cabin with its opening through the center, a loft over the dog-run for the boys to sleep in. "I swun, it's better even than what we had before. Rebecca'll be right proud."

The builders were gathering their tools and putting them in the dog-run to keep them dry. Josh leaned on his ax and admired the new structure with Aaron. "Still a right smart of finishin'-up work to be done, but I expect you and your boys can be doin' that along as you get to it."

Aaron grinned. "You fellers will all be my guests tonight. You can roll your blankets on the floor and sleep under my new roof. Once we bring the womenfolk, you ain't likely to have another chance." The grin slowly left him. "Been right concerned about the women, Josh."

"Aaron, we been back and forth over all these farms the last three-four weeks, and we ain't seen a sign."

"Sometimes the first sign you see of the Comanch is when he sends a dogwood arrow singin' at you."

"They're all right. María and the Hernandez family stayed there all by themselves while Ramón was gone to the war."

"Just the same, I'll be tickled to see Rebecca and them young'uns."

They left Quitman's wagon, for it would slow them down, and what few belongings Mrs. Winslow had could easily be carried in the Provost wagon anyway. They struck off south-westward, horseback. Homesick, Ramón held the lead. Once Josh felt compelled to catch up to him and slow him down.

"It could be dangerous, you gettin' so far out front by yourself."

Ramón said sheepishly, "I didn't notice. My mind was with Miranda and the baby. I hate to think of Miranda sleeping alone in that big, cold bed."

"You stay a little closer to the rest of us or she might sleep by herself for a long, long time."

They rode steadily through the morning, stopping at a creek to water the horses and to eat some jerked venison. Ramón was out front again as they topped the last hill and looked down on the Hernandez house. He waved his hat frantically. Josh and the others moved up in a hurry.

Ramón pointed to a blackened pile of charred timber and bones. "Josh, something has happened here."

Josh swung down and kicked at the remnants. A chill ran up his back as he counted three skulls. "Horses. Some-body's drug three dead horses up here and burned them."

Fright came into Ramón's voice. "We didn't have three horses here." Suddenly desperate, he set his mount into a hard lope.

Ramón was too far in the lead for anyone to catch him. Riding hard, Josh looked across the fields toward the house, hoping to see some sign of life. He saw none. He knew with a terrible certainty that something had gone wrong here. Then the door opened and the women hurried out under the brush arbor. The children spilled around them. Josh could see rifles in María's and Daniel's hands. *They thought we was Indians.*

Tiny Miranda ran forward to meet Ramón. Ramón slid to a stop and jumped down, grabbing her fiercely. Josh noted that Ramón's bad leg didn't seem to be bothering him much.

The dogs came running, barking. Patrick hurried out toward his father. "Daddy, Daddy, the Indians came!"

Ocie Quitman reached down and scooped the boy up into the saddle, crushing him in his arms. Quitman's voice quavered. "Son, what's that about Indians?"

"They came, Daddy, and they tried to get us."

Josh broke in, "Anybody hurt, Patrick?"

"Just Indians. María saved us, Daddy. Them old Indians was a-fixin' to get me and Daniel, but María came a-runnin'."

Quitman seemed to freeze. He stared into his son's face, dazed by the realization that he had come close to losing the boy.

Aaron Provost hugged first one of his children, then another. Rebecca waited patiently, and he squeezed her hardest of all. "Aaron, we been needin' you."

Josh dismounted slowly, his eyes on María. He reached for her hands. "María, I heard what Patrick said. Are you all right?"

She nodded, smiling. He opened his arms, drawing her to him violently. He whispered, "Thank God. If something had happened again . . ." He held her so tightly that she gasped for breath. "Sorry, María, I didn't go to hurt you. But all of a sudden I was rememberin' what happened to Teresa, a long time ago . . ."

She stiffened a little. "Nothing happened to me. Everything is fine." She dropped her head forward, against his chest. In a moment she said, "Teresa is still much on your mind, isn't she, Josh?"

He fumbled for an answer. "No, María, no. What happened here just brought it back, that's all."

The men gathered around and demanded a full account. Rebecca said, "You're the one to tell them,

María." When María shook her head, Rebecca went on, "Then I'll tell it." She gave the whole story in rousing detail.

Ocie Quitman held his son tightly. Now and again, listening, he would glance covertly at María. Patrick would break in occasionally to say, "What you scared for, Daddy? It's over with."

When Rebecca had told it all, Aaron Provost took a long, thankful look at all his children. He reached out and clasped María's fingers in one of his big hands, Heather Winslow's in the other. "You little ladies, there ain't nothin' I can say that would be half enough."

Heather put in quietly, "María did most of it."

Aaron blinked. "It beats all nature, the way a woman can come through when she has to. Girls, I know you got no daddy—either one of you—but from now on you got the next thing to a real one. If ever there comes a time you need help—no matter what or how much of it—you don't have to go no farther than the Provost house." He glanced at Josh. "Boy, you hug that girl María and do it proper. If you don't, I swear *I* will."

Ramón and Miranda heard the baby crying—or said they did—and walked into the house, arms around each other. Muley led off his and Ramón's horses, the children following after him. Aaron moved toward his wagon, one hand on Rebecca's shoulder, the other on Daniel's. Dent Sessum tramped away to examine his own wagon, fearful the Indians might have done him some damage. Josh figured he would be looking after his money, too, wherever he had hidden it. Josh said to María, "I best see after the horses. But later I'll do what Aaron said, and I'll do it right."

Ocie Quitman stared at María, even as he clung to his son. She stared after Josh, but it was evident she knew Quitman was watching her. At length she turned toward the house. Quitman said, "Miss Hernandez . . ."

She stopped. He picked around for the words, and they came with difficulty. "I need to tell you . . ."

"It's not necessary."

"This boy's the only thing I got left in the world that means anything to me. They say you saved him."

María's voice was cool. She spoke in Spanish, throwing it in his face. "If I did, it was not because he was your son. It was in spite of that. Don't hurt yourself trying to say thank you."

Stung, Quitman watched her enter the house. Patrick stuck to him like a burr as he led his horse out and turned him loose. That done, he returned to the arbor and sat on a log bench, face furrowed, his hands absently running through his son's hair. He nodded while Patrick told him again about all that had happened, coloring it with a child's fears and fantasies. The Indians had all been nine feet tall, painted and feathered and riding horses big as a house. But María had come out for him and Daniel and hadn't been scared at all. Her pony had run like the wind. At length Quitman tried to switch the subject. "What else has happened, son? What all did you do before the Indians came?"

"We hoed the fields, and we played a lot. Gregorio's my favorite, Daddy. You know Gregorio?" Quitman only nodded. The boy said eagerly, "Gregorio's goin' to teach me how to twist a rabbit out of a hole. Did you ever twist a rabbit, Daddy?" When Quitman shook his head, the boy said, "He twisted one the other day. Got it up out of its hole and caught it."

Quitman frowned. "I hope you didn't eat it? That'd be like a bunch of Mexicans."

"No, sir, Gregorio turned it loose. Said no use killin' somethin' unless it's hurtin' you or you aim to eat it. I've learned lots of things from Gregorio. He's goin' to teach me a lot more."

Quitman's gaze ranged down around the sheds, where Muley and the Provost youngsters and the Hernandez children milled. "I don't reckon he'll have the chance, son. We're fixin' to leave here."

The boy's face fell. "Leave María, and Gregorio?"

Quitman nodded. "We've built a house on the Provost place. You'll live there awhile, Patrick. Mrs. Winslow will be there too. She'll look out for you when I can't be around. She's goin' to teach all you young'uns. You'll enjoy that."

"I'd rather we was stayin' here."

"We can't. This is too far from the valley. Anyway, you like Mrs. Winslow, don't you?"

"Sure, Daddy, but I wish María and Gregorio was goin' with us too. Couldn't we take them?"

"Their home is here, son. Everybody has to live where his land is."

"I wish our land was here."

Presently Patrick ran off to join the other children. Heather Winslow came out and took another bench, near Quitman. He was frowning in disapproval as he saw his son pair up with the dark-skinned Gregorio.

Heather Winslow said, "Don't worry about it, Mister Quitman. Gregorio is all right."

"I'd just rather see Patrick take up with the Provost boys more. Better he stays with his own kind."

"It won't matter long. Aaron says we're leaving here."

"Tomorrow. We've made a place for you to live at the Provosts'. Have they talked to you about givin' the young'uns some learnin'?"

"Yes. I said I'd be glad to, as much as I can do. It's a way to help earn my keep. Anyway, there doesn't seem to be anywhere else I can go. I can't live on my place alone."

Hesitantly Quitman said, "Teachin' ain't all they got in mind. They got other plans worked out for you. And for me."

Heather blushed. "I know."

"I hope you don't let it embarrass you. Far as I'm concerned, you needn't even think about it."

She looked away. "I'll confess, Mister Quitman, I have done some thinking about it."

He stared blankly. "Come to any conclusions?"

She shook her head. "No conclusions. It's still too soon after . . . I need more time."

Quitman looked relieved. "The same with me. I'm in no mood to be pushed into somethin' by other people, no matter how good their intentions are. Whatever I decide to do—and if I do *anything*—it'll be because I made up my own mind."

"They'll keep pushing us. Rebecca keeps saying your son needs a woman's care. She keeps saying *you* need a woman, and I owe you what a woman can give."

He looked at her in surprise. "It's hard on a man, once he's been married. But don't ever feel for a minute that you owe me anything like that. You don't. I wouldn't ask you to."

Her eyes were grateful. "I know you wouldn't, Mister Quitman. But let me tell you this: if I ever decided I wanted to, you wouldn't have to ask me."

María Hernandez walked outside. She glanced a moment at Heather and Quitman, then moved out to the garden. Heather's gaze followed her. "Mister Quitman, I don't mean to tell you what you ought to do, but it would be a bad thing if you left here without telling that girl you're sorry."

"Sorry about what?"

"I shouldn't have to tell you. In spite of everything, she went out there and brought Patrick back with those devils yapping at her heels. They would've killed her if they had caught her, or they would've carried her away. If it hadn't been for her, you wouldn't have a boy."

"What can I say to her?"

Heather smiled. "You're a straightforward man, Mister Quitman. The words will come to you." Heather arose from the bench and walked down toward the Provost wagon.

Reluctantly, feeling somehow trapped, Quitman stood up. He stared at the dark-haired girl, who was pulling beans and dropping them into a tightly woven willow basket. He took a few steps toward her, stopped, clenched his fists and took a few steps more. He stood behind her, trying for words that didn't want to come. "Miss Hernandez . . ."

She turned to look at him over her shoulder. "Yes?" He stood in awkward silence. She said, "You were about to say something?"

He frowned, his fist balling up. "Yes, and I expect you know what."

"I think so. I can see the pain in your face. It hurts."

"Like pullin' out my own teeth."

"Then forget about it, Mister Quitman."

"No. I always been one to pay my debts."

"I am just a Mexican. You have said so. You owe me nothing."

A touch of anger came, and he wasn't sure whether it was at her or at himself. "Yes, you're a Mexican. I won't lie about it: that's what makes it so hard for me to say. But I *will* say it if it kills me. I oughtn't to've treated you the way I done. I reckon it ain't your fault bein' born what you was. And what you done for my boy leaves me a debt I can never pay you for."

Her eyes were hard. "I think you resent that it was me. You wish it had been anybody else—Heather Winslow, or Rebecca—anybody but this Mexican girl."

His face pinched. "You see right through a man, don't you?" He shrugged. "I reckon you got cause to hate me, but that's the way it is. I can't help the way I feel. I can't cover it up and act like it ain't there."

Some of the harsh dislike faded from her eyes. She looked at him strangely. "That is true, Mister Quitman. You can't, and you don't try. There are some who smile and talk nice but hate inside. You are not one of those." She looked down at the willow basket. "She must have been a good woman, your wife."

His voice tightened. "Yes, she was."

"I am sorry you lost her."

"It had nothin' to do with you. I got no reason to make you share the blame for it. It's just somethin' inside me I can't control. I can apologize for it, but I can't stop it."

"Then the best thing is for you to stay away . . . from all my people."

"That's what I been tryin' to do. Luck just keeps throwin' us together. And now I'm owin' you . . ."

"I do not accept the debt. Some of my people did you a bad wrong. Whatever I did, take it as a payment on what my people owe to *you*."

She carried the basket back to the house. He watched till she passed through the door and out of view. He stopped to pick up a long string bean she had dropped, and he shifted his gaze down to the shed where Buckalew was.

He remembered then the talk of Buckalew marrying this girl. He thought, *Maybe Buckalew isn't as far wrong as I figured him.*

XI

I**T WAS A BUSY SUMMER, FOR THERE WERE NOT ONLY THE** crops to be weeded and garden plots to be tended and stock to be worked, but there was also all the rebuilding to be done, the war scars to be rubbed away with muscle strain and sweat and determination. Josh's cattle had scattered. Many were completely gone, taken perhaps by beef-hungry Mexican troops. In the unsettled country to the west roamed wild cattle, descended in freedom from those which had strayed long ago out of the Spanish mission herds. These cattle were spotted and striped and every color a man had ever seen, their horns long and their legs longer. They fleshened well on grass and were far less gamey than the wild deer and turkey and bear which kept so many settlers' ribs from showing through the skin. Brought home, gentled enough to stay, they would be good for trading in the settlements. When they had time, Josh and Muley and Ramón and Gregorio rode west, picking up wild cattle where they could find them. Often they had to rope them with rawhide *reatas* and throw them down and tie up a leg to slow them and make them workable. Sometimes they necked them to gentler cattle brought along

from home. Slowly through the summer they built their
herds by going out and bringing in what Nature had pro-
vided. Some cattle they kept; some strayed right back
where they had come from.

There was this about early Texas: if it *was* a big and un-
tamed land, and if its people *were* poor and ragged and ever
standing in the presence of danger, at least Nature herself
was bountiful. No man went hungry if he had a horse and a
rope, or if he had a rifle and powder and ball, or if he had
the knowledge and material to build even a snare.

When they weren't after cattle, Josh and Muley and
Ramón were sometimes out searching for the mustangs
which roamed these hills and valleys in numbers beyond
counting. They built wings and traps and hazed the horses
into them, then caught them Mexican style with their heavy
rawhide *reatas* and brought them to hand. These were
grand days, these fleeting days of summer, and it pleased
Josh that Ramón was once more learning to laugh. It was
not the high, easy laughter of the old days, but that would
never come back. That was killed forever. Even the little
chuckle that followed a good ride on a mustang bronc was
an improvement, though, and Josh was gratified.

They spent so much time gentling these captured horses
that summer was far gone before Josh realized they had not
made any preparations for building a cabin. They'd slept in
the open through the warm weather, but he and Muley
would need tight walls and a roof before the fall northers
began moving in with the chilling bite of raw prairie wind.

After the corn crop was harvested, Josh and Muley
started looking for cabin timber. They chopped down trees,
stripped off the branches and dragged in logs at the end of
a *reata*. As he could, Josh measured off the size the structure was to be and started cutting and shaping the logs,
notching the ends to fit together. He fashioned this cabin
bigger than his old one had been, for in the back of his

mind was the notion that one day he would bring María here to live. He would ask her someday, when he had the place fixed up the way he wanted it, the way it ought to be for a woman. A man could live in any kind of a house, so long as it kept the rain off of his head. But he couldn't expect a woman to live that way, not if he had any real feeling for her.

Because his crop was the earliest in, Josh had shared his corn. He hauled roasting ears to the neighbors. Later, as the ears hardened, he had carried grinding corn to the Provosts and Mrs. Winslow and Quitman, and Jacob Phipps. He had even given some to Dent Sessum and Alfred Noonan, living like a pair of boar hogs in the squalor of old Noonan's place. This, with the game they killed, saw the settlers through until their own crops could ripen.

In return, they owed Josh and Muley a cabin-raising. They would have done it debt or not—all, perhaps, but Sessum and Noonan. Those damned reprobates didn't seem to feel they owed anybody anything. Josh was surprised to see Sessum and Noonan ride in the morning everybody was to gather and start raising the cabin. He was not made joyful by their coming. Nevertheless, he tried to be civil.

"Didn't figure I'd see you-all." He might have added that the only time he *ever* saw them was when he took them something, like the roasting ears.

"Never miss a cabin-raisin'," Noonan enthused. "Been to many a one in my day. I do hope you got some drinkin'-whisky. Me and Sessum, we been whettin' our bills."

Josh hesitated to admit it. He and Muley had taken some cattle down into the settlements for trade and had come back with several jugs of whisky, among other things. It would be neighborly to furnish an occasional snort to friends helping bring up a cabin. He told the old man, "I expect we can dig up a swig or two when the time comes."

"It's always time," Noonan said. But Josh didn't offer.

Sessum said, "Buckalew, you got somethin' me and Noonan could be doin' to help you?" He didn't sound particularly eager, but maybe he thought it would help hurry the whisky. Josh decided to see how much work he might get out of them. He knew they would get plenty of his whisky.

"We'll need more clapboards for the roof. I got logs sawed for the job if you-all would like to rive them for me."

Normally one man could rive logs, but Sessum and Noonan made a two-man job of it. They would place the sharp edge of the froe on the upended short log and drive it down by pounding on its blunt upper edge with a wooden hammer, splitting off a board about an inch thick. The rate they started, Josh calculated they could spend a week. But it would keep them out from under foot.

"Where's Jacob Phipps?" he asked. "Surprised you didn't bring him."

Old Noonan grunted. "Tell you the truth, Josh, I been a mite disappointed in him. He ain't been none too friendly of late. You know one day he even had the gall to tell me and Sessum to git ourselves off of his place? And us old friends, the way we was. I swear, you can't put your faith in nobody anymore."

The war had cost Phipps an arm, Josh thought, but it seemed to have sharpened his judgment. He asked Sessum, "How about you? Still huntin' you a place to buy?"

Sessum shook his head. "I still got my eye on the place your Mexican friend has got, if he'd just talk business."

In Josh's view, the thing that had drawn Sessum's interest at Ramón's was the neatness of it, the way the fields were clean-worked and the crops coming along well. Sessum didn't recognize the work that had gone into it to get it that way, and the work it would take to maintain it in that condition. If a man like Sessum got hold of it, the place would look like a disaster had struck inside of six months. "Ramón won't sell. You'd just as well forget it."

Sessum shrugged. "Man never can tell what may happen. The Mexicans are liable to decide they want to leave, and I'll be in a position to buy."

"They been here longer than any of us. Nothin' is apt to change their minds. You leave them alone, Sessum. You'll likely find somebody else willin' to sell, if you'll look around."

"I been watchin' Jacob Phipps. He's havin' hell tryin' to work that place of his with just one good arm. I figure one of these days he'll give up and take an offer. Who knows? I might be able to buy his land and the Hernandez place both if they go cheap enough. You'd have me for a neighbor on both sides of you, Buckalew."

Josh turned away, scowling. He'd as soon have a Comanche village on one flank and the cannibalistic Karankawans on the other.

A couple of horses showed up to the west, and a high-wheeled Mexican cart drawn by mules. Ramón Hernandez led the way on a big, brown horse. He was bringing the whole family—Miranda, the baby, María, and all the brothers and sisters. Hickory loped out to greet them, barking all the way. From east came Aaron and Rebecca Provost in their wagon, bringing with them Mrs. Winslow and Patrick and all the young Provosts. Ocie Quitman rode alongside with lanky Daniel Provost. Their dogs bounced in front of them, setting up a barking contest with Hickory. The Provost children jumped out of their wagon and raced toward the Hernandez family. Patrick climbed down shouting, "Gregorio! Hey, Gregorio!" Quitman tried to stop him, but the boy was away like a deer.

It took a while for everybody to get through with the hugging and the howdying. Presently the women hauled

out their cooking utensils and took a critical look at a side
of beef which had been placed over the coals early in the
morning. Josh and Muley squatted on their heels with
Aaron and Ramón to swap talk. Pretty soon Muley became
bored with it all and trailed off after the youngsters. Ocie
Quitman listened, but his gaze absently followed the
women.

Been a long time now since he lost his wife, Josh thought.
*Nature's starting to work on him. He's probably gone to
thinking more and more about Heather Winslow. And he
ought to. She's a right handsome woman.*

Old Noonan came around and began wedging into the
conversation. And once he started, he had a way of taking
it over, asking the questions and giving the answers. One
by one the men commenced getting up and looking for
work to do. The foundation logs went down first. Then the
builders started "rolling up" the side walls. By dusk, when
Josh called a halt, they had the project well started. They
were a long way from reaching the roofline, but the women
would have a place to sleep tonight, "indoors."

Off and on during the day, as appetite hit them, the men
had gone to the beef, slicing hot strips of barbecue from
the carcass which had slow-cooked over the gentle heat of
the coals. Now the women were preparing a regular supper.
The smoke from their fire smelled good to Josh, for his
stomach growled in complaint, and his muscles ached from
straining with the heavy logs. He took a cup and walked to
the fire, where Heather Winslow was stirring beans in a
pot. He filled the cup with coffee and paused to visit a little.

"How's the school comin', Mrs. Winslow?"

"Not good, not bad. We just have to make do with what
little we've got. Do you know we have only two books for
the children to learn from? The Bible and *Pilgrim's
Progress*. We have a copy of the United States Constitu-
tion, too, but we never got past the part about the pursuit of

happiness. Daniel Provost said he's pursued deer, but he didn't know you had to pursue happiness. He'd never seen it run."

She smiled, but Josh didn't. It didn't strike him that way. He said, "Happiness is a hard thing to catch hold of, sometimes. Maybe it don't run, exactly, but it's got a habit of slippin' away from you."

"This ought to be a happy place you have here, Mister Buckalew. I like the way the creek lies, and all those trees. I like the view as you stand here and look off to the south and east. It will be a good place to bring a woman." She nodded toward the cabin. "It's going to be a big one. Of course you'll have to find a place to put Muley, once María comes here to live."

"I'll build him another cabin."

"You sound as if you already have your plans made."

"I done a lot of studyin'."

"Then maybe you ought to talk with María. I gather that she's not sure what your intentions are."

"I figured they've always been understood without me sayin'."

"By you, maybe, but not by her, Mister Buckalew. A woman doesn't like things taken for granted. She wants to hear them said out loud."

He grimaced. "Truth is, Mrs. Winslow, I never have been around women much. I had some sisters, but they was older, and I never did understand them anyway. They all cussed about men, then up and married the first ones that come along and asked them. María . . . she was not much more than a little girl first time I ever saw her. I reckon that's the way I've thought of her, till just lately."

"Till you realized all of a sudden that she was a grown woman, like her sister had been?"

He stared into the coffee. "I rode up to their house one day, and for a minute I would've sworn she was Teresa. It was like all the years had rolled away and Teresa had come back from the long ago. You've got no idea the way I felt."

Heather Winslow mused, "I can imagine. It would be as if Jim were to ride in here right now, come back to life." She frowned, "It could happen, you know . . . I mean, somebody could come along who looked like Jim, who talked like him. But it wouldn't *be* Jim. Nobody else could ever be him, no matter how much he looked like him, or how much I wanted him to be. Jim's dead. There's no use me looking for him."

Josh studied her over the cup. "Is the teacher tryin' to teach *me* somethin'?"

"Just this, Mister Buckalew: María is a woman with a love in her, and she'd be good for a man who really loved her. But a person who has room for so much love also has room for a lot of hurt. Don't you hurt her."

"I wouldn't for the world."

"You might, and not mean to. Be careful with her, Mister Buckalew."

After supper, María took a bucket and walked down toward the creek in the near darkness. Ocie Quitman sat on his heels by a small campfire, old Noonan's incessant rattling falling upon his ears but not penetrating the mental shield Quitman had raised. He watched the girl go out of sight over the creekbank. Quitman pushed to his feet, stretched, then began moving toward the line of trees, taking his time as if he had no place to go, nothing to do but exercise his legs. He walked down the creek bank and met María starting up, straining. "That looks heavy," he said. "I'll carry it for you."

She stood frozen in surprise, the bucket at arm's length. He said again, "I'll take it."

"Why?"

"I told you. It's too heavy."

"I've been carrying buckets like this for years. I'll carry them the rest of my life."

"Well, I'll carry this one." He reached for it, and she gave it to him. He made no move to start up the bank, however. She stared, her eyes still showing surprise.

Finally she said experimentally, "How have you been, Mister Quitman?"

"All right. Been workin' awful hard."

"It seems to do you good. You look well."

"I look like a tired man older than I really am. But work's good for a man, especially if he's got heavy things on his mind. Keeps him too busy to worry much, or grieve. Work's a good healer."

"I suppose."

Frowning, he looked away from her. "Miss Hernandez, I followed you down here on purpose."

"For what reason?"

"To talk to you, to unload a little bit of guilt, maybe. I've said things I'm not proud of. I been wantin' you to know. I carried an awful anger, before. I've worked a lot of it off, I think."

"Have you changed your thinking, about . . . *things?*"

He shook his head. "I wouldn't lie to you. Some things burn so deep in a man that he can't root them out, no matter how much he'd like to. But I want you to know I'm sorry for the pain I've caused you. I had no right."

"I have no grudge against you, Mister Quitman."

"I didn't have the right. It was just in me to hurt you . . . to hurt *all* of you."

She shrugged. "That's all behind us. Anyway, you apologized before."

"The way I apologized was an insult in itself. I didn't mean it, and you could tell I didn't. Now I *do* mean it."

Her narrowed eyes held to his for a long time before a

faint smile tugged at her mouth. He was hunched over, leaning strongly to the side where he held the bucket of water.

"That looks heavy, Mister Quitman. Maybe you should let me carry it."

He eased at the sight of her smile. A tiny hint of one crossed his face and disappeared, for smiling did not come easily to Ocie Quitman. "You've just taken a heavy load off of my shoulders, Miss Hernandez. I reckon I can carry the bucket."

Josh kept the jugs hidden out and fetched them one at a time at a deliberate rate calculated to keep anyone from getting drunk. There was no stopping old man Noonan, though. For every swallow anyone else took, he took three. His Adam's apple bobbed up and down several times with each lifting of the jug. The more he drank, the wilder, louder and more continuously he talked. It occurred to Josh finally that the old scoundrel probably had found his jug cache, so he had Muley slip out and move it. Surely enough, they were one jug shy. Old Noonan was hiding it out.

Against his protests Josh found the cabin getting completely out of hand. Aaron Provost virtually took over the project. What Josh had seen as a two-day job turned into quite a bit more, and his envisioned one-room cabin became a big double cabin with a liberal dog-run separating the two halves, one common roof over the whole structure. When the roof finally went up, it didn't lack much being as big as the one they had built for the Provosts.

To all of Josh's protests, Aaron waved his hand in dismissal. "One fine day you'll be bringin' María home to this place, and first thing you know there'll be some black-headed young'uns runnin' around and we'd all have to come back over and build it bigger anyway. Just as well do it now when we won't be in the way of nothin'.''

So, up it went. The one-armed Jacob Phipps mixed mortar and fitted stone and put up a fireplace in each section of the cabin, smiling in pride as he backed away to admire his handiwork. This was something he could do and do well despite the handicap war had thrust upon him.

Noonan and Sessum were out of sight half the time, sleeping on the creek bank. Noonan, in particular, had a lot to sleep off.

When the cabin was finished, Aaron Provost gathered the others around him and walked out a hundred feet, turning to look back in the dusk. He made a sweeping gesture with his hand. "What it lacks for purty, it sure makes up for stout. You can live to be a hundred and six, Josh, but you'll never have a better house."

Josh nodded his appreciation. "I don't know why I'd ever *want* a better one. All I can say is thank you."

"You're welcome. We owed it to you, and by johnny there can't nobody say a Texan don't pay his debts. It's all complete, Josh, floor to the roof. Got fireplaces, got tables and benches and a bed. All you lack now is a woman to put in it. That's somethin' you'll just have to take care of for yourself." Aaron squeezed María's shoulder. She looked down, her face reddening.

"There'll be time enough," Josh said.

"Not as much as you think, maybe," Aaron responded. "Winter's comin'. Fireplace ain't goin' to be enough to keep you warm."

Ocie Quitman watched María's face, and his eyebrows furrowed as he listened to Aaron's good-natured joking.

Aaron said, "Josh, you still got another jug hid out?"

"Just one more. That's all that's left."

"Let's get it, then. No house is finished proper till the

builders have had them a chance to take a drink under its roof." Aaron put his arm around Josh's shoulder and pulled him toward the cabin. The others followed. Only María waited there, and Quitman. She stared at the new cabin, her dark eyes beginning to glisten.

Quitman's voice was quiet. "You oughtn't to be sheddin' tears, Miss Hernandez. It's a good house. From what I hear, it's goin' to be yours."

She shook her head. "That's what everybody says. Everybody but Josh."

"He hasn't asked you?"

"No."

"You want him to?"

She cut her gaze to him a moment. "For a long time I've wanted him to. Now I'm not sure anymore."

"I thought you were in love with him."

"I thought so too. I've thought so ever since I was a girl. But love has to come from two people . . . it can't be all with one."

"You don't think he loves you?"

"I think he thinks he does. But it isn't really me. It never was."

Quitman found himself walking slowly toward the cabin, beside her. Worriedly he asked, "So, what're you goin' to do about it?"

"What *can* I do? Wait till he asks me, then tell him we've both been wrong."

"It'll be a disappointment to him."

"At first, till he realizes I'm right."

"And this cabin, that's been built for you?"

"There will be another woman sometime, one who doesn't look like my sister Teresa . . . one he can love for herself and not for somebody else."

They were at the side of the cabin now. Quitman halted, hands flexing nervously. "María . . ." He broke off. Always before he had called her Miss Hernandez, if he had given her a name at all.

She turned. "Yes?"

"María, I lost somebody once. She didn't look anything like you." His chin dropped, and he groped for the right words. "I don't hardly know how to say it . . ."

Her face pinched. "I think I know what you're trying to say. Be careful . . ."

"María, I wronged you, and I worried over it. I couldn't figure out why it ought to bother me so much. The last few days here, seein' you all the time, I knew why."

"Mister Quitman, don't . . ."

"You got every cause to hate me; I got no right to expect anything else. And if I told you I'd lost all the feelin' I've had against your people, I'd be lyin' to you. But damn it, María, in spite of all that . . ."

She stared at him in painful silence.

He said, "The last few days I've fought it. My eyes have followed you everywhere you moved, and I've fought it. I didn't noway want it to happen, but it's happened anyhow. So, help me, María. Curse me . . . hit me. Do somethin' to make me stop bein' in love with you."

She said quietly, "I'm not sure I want to."

"It isn't any good. I oughtn't to've told you."

"You didn't have to. I've sensed it as long as you have."

"You must've been laughin' at me."

"No, it wasn't funny."

"Then you must've hated me."

Her fingers reached out and gently closed over his hand. "I don't hate you. I never did."

He took a step forward, close to her. He reached a hand behind her neck and pulled her toward him, bending. Her face turned upward, and her eyes closed as he found her lips. He kissed her with a cautious gentleness. Her arms went around him, and her mouth pressed tighter, and he cast away the caution, the gentleness. He let loose the pent-up anger and the hunger and the aching loneliness that had built so long. She gasped for breath.

A sharp voice jerked him back and brought him halfway around.

"María!"

Joshua Buckalew stood at the corner, face creased in surprise. "Quitman, what in the . . ."

Ocie Quitman turned loose of the girl and faced Josh. Josh seemed frozen in his tracks. Then he moved, fists clenched.

Quitman said, "Buckalew, it ain't like it looks . . ."

"Ain't it? María, you go in the cabin. He ain't goin' to bother you no more."

María didn't move. Her eyes were big and dark and frightened.

Josh swung his fist. It struck Quitman solidly on the chin and he staggered back into María. She tried to grab him, but he fell, almost tripping her when he went down. She cried out as Josh reached down to grab Quitman's shirt and haul him back to his feet. She grasped at Josh's hands. "Josh, don't do it . . . Don't . . ."

Josh wasn't listening to her. "Damn your soul, Quitman! After all the things you've said . . . and then you try to take her like this. I'll beat you to death."

María had hold of Josh's arm. "Josh, listen to me . . ."

Josh pulled away from her and struck Quitman again, sending him stumbling backward into the log wall. Quitman hunched there, shaking his head, clearing his eyes. Then the anger rushed into his face and he surged out swinging. The two men rammed into each other like a pair of bulls fighting. Arms muscled by hard work, hands toughened by rain and wind and sun, they swung and pounded and slashed and jabbed, one pushing awhile, the other giving ground, then reversing. They circled and fell

and rolled and pushed to their feet and pounded again until
their shirts hung in ribbons and blood streaked their faces
like Indian war paint. They grunted and cursed and shouted
in their anger. One went to his knees, and then the other.
They fought until they were far out from the cabin, almost
to the bank of the creek. At the end they were staggering,
and each man almost fell every time he swung. Ocie Quitman finally stumbled and went to his knees and couldn't
come up anymore. Josh teetered on the edge of the bank,
trying to keep his footing, trying to focus his eyes, trying to
find Quitman one more time.

Aaron Provost's strong voice broke through to him. "Josh,
for God's sake, don't you think there's been enough?"

María Hernandez cried, "Josh, it's over."

Josh gritted stubbornly, "Where's he at?"

In fury María gave Josh a push that sent him stumbling
backward over the bank and into the cold water of the
creek. He splashed and floundered, sputtering. "There!"
she cried. "Cool off a little!"

Weeping, she knelt to try to help Ocie Quitman to his
feet. Bewildered, Ramón came to her aid. He got Quitman
up, staggering. Aaron Provost strode over the bank and
climbed down to extend a huge hand to Josh. "Boy, I got no
idea what's happened between you two, but you sure have
tore each other up. This is a hell of a way to celebrate a
new cabin."

Jug in his hand, old Noonan was snickering to Dent Sessum. "It's that gal, Dent. They'll do it every time. I been
knowin' Mexican gals for years and years, and that's the
way they'll do you. Hug and kiss and sweet-do you while
you're there, and the minute you're out of sight they're
flashin' their eyes at somebody else."

Ramón Hernandez reached down for a handful of mud
from the edge of an old rain puddle. Noonan's mouth was
wide open when Ramón came up with his hand and

plopped the mud in. The old man coughed and spluttered and cursed.

Aaron brought Josh up out of the creek. Ocie Quitman waited there, leaning on María's thin shoulder for strength. Their eyes met, anger still crackling in Josh's. But the anger had burned out of Quitman. The ashes held only a cold regret.

"I didn't mean it to happen, Buckalew. But God help me, I'm in love with your Mexican girl."

XII

THE FESTIVE MOOD WHICH HAD LASTED THROUGH the building of the cabin was gone like summer smoke. Even the children sensed the change and bedded down quietly, the play gone out of them. Ocie Quitman moved his bedroll out beyond anyone else's, and though he awakened with morning's first light and rolled up his blankets, he made no move toward the house. He sat out there alone, brooding, his gaze lost in the light fog which masked off the sunrise.

Old Alfred Noonan held his head in his hands as he raised up in his blankets beside the corral and watched Quitman, half hoping there might be another fight but knowing there wouldn't be. That was why Quitman was staying out there by himself.

"Damn," Noonan complained hoarsely, "looks like Buckalew could've got a better grade of drinkin'-whisky, us buildin' him a cabin and all."

Dent Sessum only groaned and turned over. Noonan pushed him with his foot. "Dent, stir yourself."

Sessum raised up irritably, blinking in a sleepy confusion. "What the hell's the matter?"

Noonan shook his head. "Ain't nothin' the matter. All of a sudden I got me a notion things is fixin' to get better." He could see Ramón Hernandez up and moving around, loading his high-wheeled cart.

Sessum rubbed his forehead and whispered some choice words about how it felt like somebody was splitting his head with a chopping ax.

Noonan growled. "You ain't no worse off than me. I got an awful taste in my mouth this mornin'. Can't figure out whether it's like bad whisky or black mud."

"Mud, likely. You got the Mexican to thank for that."

Noonan scowled and cut a hard glance toward the distant Ramón. "And I do intend to thank him good and proper. Man can't go around lettin' them chili-eaters get away with insults, or first thing you know they'll think they own this country again."

Sessum's eyes were rimmed with red. "What you intend to do about it?"

Noonan looked around him furtively. "Dent, I think I've figured out somethin' that'll be good for both of us. Me, I got a grudge to settle with Ramón, and anyway, I just don't like Mexicans. You, you been wantin' to buy that piece of land from him but he won't listen. I bet his *widow* would listen."

"He ain't got no widow."

"He's fixin' to have. It could happen today . . . this very mornin'."

Sessum blinked, trying to absorb the meaning of it all, but it was too big for him.

Noonan said, "Everybody's had Indians on the brain since that raid over at the Hernandez place. Now, if somebody was to shoot Ramón, who do you reckon would catch the blame for it?"

"The Comanch."

"You're soberin' up, Dent. Now, the way I see it, them

Mexicans'll eat breakfast pretty soon and start home. Way things went to hell here last night, they'll be wantin' to leave. We could do the same, only we could double back, ride in the creek aways to lose our tracks, then lay in wait where the brush comes up close to the trail. After it's done, we just follow the creek till we lose our tracks again, then we go on home with nobody the wiser, and Ramón Hernandez a hell of a lot deader."

"What'll Jacob Phipps think?"

"He don't need to know. We come here without him; we can leave without him."

Sessum rubbed his chin, his eyes gradually coming alive. "It's a pleasure to know you, Noonan. I'm proud to ride with a man who uses his head for somethin' besides a place to put his hat. You goin' to give me first shot?"

"Think you're sober enough to hit him?"

"I'll *be* sober enough, if there's one more drink left in that jug." Sessum pawed around beneath the blankets. Finding the jug, he tipped it up and shook it. But they'd been too diligent the night before. It was empty.

Sourly Noonan said, "Looks like a host would see to it he had enough whisky so a man didn't run out."

As a smuggler and a filibusterer in Texas even before the days of Stephen F. Austin, old Noonan had done his share of fighting against Mexican soldiers and customs officers as well as against Indians. When Dent Sessum started to tie his horse in the brush, the old man impatiently grabbed the reins. "Damn it, Dent, you're as green as a gourd vine. Your horse is liable to jerk loose when the shootin' starts and leave you afoot. Tie a rope to your reins and hang onto it. That way you always got hold of him."

Noonan showed Sessum how to tie a length of rawhide *reata* to his reins, then loop the end over his arm. "A horse is lots of things, but smart ain't one of them. He don't like a rifle goin' off in his face. This way you get far enough from him that he don't spook so bad. You got both arms free, and still you don't let him run loose."

A thin fog still clung to the ground and obscured the view of anything more than fifty yards away. They crouched a long time in the brush, till Dent Sessum's legs went stiff. His fingers played nervously up and down the stock of his long rifle. "Sure do wish I had me another jug."

"You'd be drinkin' out of it, and you couldn't shoot straight."

"Why don't they hurry up and come on? You sure we got out ahead of them, Noonan? They could've already passed this way."

Noonan gritted, "Calm down, Dent. You're gettin' the shakes, and that ain't goin' to help none. They'll be along directly."

Sessum hunched his shoulders. "I swear it's gettin' cold. Fall ain't far enough along for it to be this cold."

"It's just you. You got the trembles from that whisky wearin' off. Scared, Dent?"

"What I got to be scared of?"

"Nothin'. That's what I'm tryin' to tell you. A Mexican's easy to kill. Just send a bullet whistlin' by his ear and he'll die of fright."

"That ain't the way I heard tell about the war."

"Folks lie. There ain't nothin' to killin' a Mexican. You'll see. Square yourself up."

From east it came, out of the fog, the wailing of wooden wheels rubbing against a wooden axle. Noonan turned in triumph. "See what I told you, Dent? You can hear one of them Mexican carts a mile away. Now, you get ahold of yourself."

They crouched lower and waited. Sessum's hands still played nervously up and down the rifle stock and on the barrel. Cold sweat popped out on his forehead, and he rubbed his sleeved arm across his face.

Noonan turned and frowned at him. "Dent, you sure you still want the first shot? Maybe I better take it."

Sessum shook his head. "I've took a right smart off of him too. I've took it off *all* of them. I want my bullet in him first."

Noonan shrugged. "All right, but don't you miss."

The groaning of the wheels came louder. Both men squinted and tried to see into the fog. Sessum's tongue darted back and forth across dry lips, and again he rubbed his sleeve over his face.

Noonan pointed. "There they come. You can see them now."

Ramón Hernandez rode his brown horse a little in front of the cart. He held a rifle balanced across his lap. His head moved slowly from left to right as his gaze swept the patches of brush that lay on either side of the trail. It touched the thick oak where Noonan and Sessum crouched, but they were hidden by the heavy green foliage.

The two Mexican women and the children rode in the cart, all but the boy Gregorio. He trailed behind, a-horse-back. In his hands was an old blunderbuss.

Noonan whispered, "Now, Dent, you just move slow, and don't be in no hurry. He'll be in your sights plenty long enough."

Sessum licked his lips nervously and leveled the rifle, resting its long barrel across a limb. He blinked hard, turned his cheek to wipe the sweat onto his shoulder, then returned to the sights. His hands trembled.

"Wait, Dent . . ." Noonan warned. "You're goin' to miss."

But Sessum jerked the trigger. The rifle belched.

Noonan spat in disgust. "See there, Dent, I told you; you missed him." Noonan brought his own rifle into line. The children were screaming, and Ramón reined around to lope

back to the cart. In the swirling confusion Noonan took
aim at what he thought was Ramón. After the roar of the rifle, he heard a high-pitched scream. Through the black
smoke he saw a small figure lurch forward in the cart. "Hit
one of the women," Noonan hissed. The horses danced in
fright, jerking against the reins looped over Noonan's and
Sessum's arms.

A ball tore through the leaves over their heads. Noonan
gritted, "He'll be comin' in a minute, that Mexican. If he
sees us, we'll have to kill them all."

"What'll we do?"

"We've spilt our chance. We better be gettin' the hell up
and gone."

Rifles still empty, they swung onto the horses and moved
out in a lope. Noonan looked back over his shoulder,
thankful for the fog. "One good thing," he muttered, "he'll
move cautious, thinkin' we was a passel of Indians. It'll
give us time to clear out."

They rode in a hard run for a few hundred yards, then
slowed to an easier lope to spare the horses. After a couple
of miles they gradually came to a stop. Noonan turned his
head so that his right ear was toward the direction from
which they had come.

Sessum asked anxiously, "Hear anything?"

"Only you. My old ears ain't the best anyhow. Maybe
you better listen for both of us."

Sessum stood in the stirrups, turning his head slowly.
"Quiet as a grave."

Noonan nodded in satisfaction. "Didn't figure he'd come
chasin' us and leave the women and kids. Especially, him
not knowin' but what we was Indians."

Sessum frowned. "I seen that woman fall. You shot her
instead of Ramón, didn't you?"

Noonan shrugged. "Ain't no way to tell. Never pleasured
me none to kill a woman, but them Mexican women breed

more little ones anyway, and little ones grow into big ones, and we'd just have to kill them someday."

They rode west until they struck a creek, then rode down the bank into the water. They rode in the water's edge for a couple of miles, glancing back occasionally for sign of pursuit. Noonan saw no reason there ought to be, and he found no evidence of any.

Finally he said "I reckon we been far enough. Let's get up out of this creek and head for home."

"Suits me," Sessum replied, and reined his horse around. He touched spurs to him and climbed up the steep bank, Noonan trailing. As he reached the top, Sessum suddenly jerked on the reins.

"Noonan!" he shouted in terror.

An arrow thumped into his chest and drove halfway through. Before he had time to fall, another arrow thudded between his ribs. His eyes rolled back and he slipped out of the saddle, tumbling, skidding, sliding down the muddy bank.

Sessum's horse lost its footing and slid back into Noonan's with an impact that jarred the old man loose from the saddle. Still gripping his rifle, he slammed against the muddy ground and pushed himself to his feet. He grabbed at the reins, but the horse broke away from him and ran. He shouted at Sessum's horse, which almost ran him down in its mad break to escape.

Mouth open, Noonan stood on wobbly legs and stared in helpless fear at the half dozen riders who suddenly towered above him on the creekbank. He got a glimpse of feathers and bare chests and bows, of gotch-eared ponies and bull-hide shields. He raised the rifle and remembered he never had taken time to reload it. Dropping it, he turned to run in the soft mud. A sharp pain stopped him in midstride. He grabbed at his side and felt his fingers clasp the shaft of an arrow, imbedded between his ribs. The numbness passed and the pain rushed on with the sudden intensity of hellfire. He tried again to run but found his legs would not bend, his feet would not move. He heard the thump of another arrow and felt it like the blow of a huge hammer against his back.

Twisting half around, Noonan stared in wordless horror at the warrior heeling his pony down the bank and coming at him in a run. He stared in deadly fascination at the heavy stone ax in the Indian's hand. He saw the strong brown arm come up. His eyes followed the downward arc of the stone as it swung savagely toward his head. The last sound he heard was his own terrified scream.

XIII

HEATHER WINSLOW CAME BACK INTO THE CABIN WITH a plate and an empty coffee cup. She was shaking her head. "Mister Quitman didn't eat much. Said he wasn't hungry. Drank the coffee, was about all."

Joshua Buckalew sat frowning down at his heavy cowhide boots. He said nothing.

Heather added, "He wants to know how long before we're ready to leave. He's impatient."

Aaron Provost grunted and turned to look sharply at Josh. "Ain't no use you two partin' with this thing hangin' over you. Sooner or later you both got to come to some understandin'. Why not start now and get done with it?"

Irritably Josh said, "What's there to talk about? We try to talk, like as not we'll end up fightin' again. He done what he done, and that's all there is to it."

Aaron argued, "He didn't go to. You ought to know him well enough to realize that of all the women on earth, María would be one of the last he'd want to fall in love with. Man just can't always help himself."

Josh arose and impatiently slapped a hand against his hip. "The whole subject pains me. I'd as soon not talk no more."

Aaron shrugged. He glanced around for his wife. "Rebecca, you got them kids about all ready to go? No use us wastin' any more time around here. It's a long ways."

"You and the boys can load the wagon," she said, her level gaze on Josh rather than on her husband. Josh couldn't tell whether she sympathized with him or blamed him. In the lingering of hurt and anger, he couldn't bring himself to care much.

He said, "I appreciate all you done, buildin' me this cabin. I'm sorry things went to hell at the last."

Aaron grimaced. "Life's thataway. 'Bout the time you figure you finally got everything on a downhill pull, somethin' comes along and stands you on your head." He walked out of the cabin, paused in the dog-run to frown at the lingering fog, then strode on out into the yard, hollering orders at the young ones. Most times Josh would have helped them tote their goods to the wagon, but this morning it wasn't in him. He leaned against the log wall and watched disconsolately. He hated to see them all leave; yet, he wanted to be alone awhile, to think things clear. A man couldn't study a problem out with people waiting around to hear what his decision was.

Josh cast a glance toward Ocie Quitman, who sat on his rolled blankets way out yonder. His fists knotted, and he found them painfully sore. *Dammit,* he thought with a surge of self-anger, *keep control of yourself. The world hasn't come to an end yet.*

It came to him that Aaron had been right about one thing. Feeling the way he did about Mexican people, Ocie Quitman wouldn't have wanted to let himself develop any feeling for María Hernandez . . . not even a passing physical desire, much less anything stronger or more lasting. Josh let his gaze follow Quitman as the man pushed to his feet and began to pace restlessly. *Bet he feels guilty about*

*the whole thing. The kind of pride he's got, it probably tor-
ments his soul to find out just how human he really is.*

Under other circumstances, Josh might have found it in
himself to pity Quitman, even. If it had been some other
Mexican girl . . . But not María. *He's not good enough for
her. After all the things he's said, he's not fit to walk the
same ground where she's been.*

Daniel Provost brought up the horses and began to help
Aaron harness the team. Ocie Quitman came near the
cabin for the first time and saddled his own horse. He carefully avoided looking at Josh.

Heather Winslow stopped beside Joshua Buckalew and
fidgeted, plainly wanting to say something but finding
nothing that didn't sound hollow to her. "It's a good house,
Mister Buckalew. And this thing with María . . . you'll get
it straightened out. I never met a better girl."

"Thank you." He was surprised at the hoarseness of his
voice. "I'm sorry you had to be around and see it. I expect you were disappointed with Ocie Quitman . . . and
with me."

"I'll live over it, Mister Buckalew. And so will you."

She walked out to the wagon and helped Patrick Quitman up into the bed of it, with the Provost youngsters. Muley stood there, sadly telling them all goodbye. Aaron
Provost gave each of the two women a lift up, then placed
his foot on the right front wheel and swung his big frame
onto the seat. "Come over when you can, Josh. We'll shoot
a fat doe." He hollered at the team, and the wagon began to
roll.

Ocie Quitman sat on his horse, waiting for the wagon to
come even with him. When it did, he pulled in beside it,
Daniel Provost a horseback on the other side. Quitman
looked back over his shoulder at Josh. He rode a few yards,
pulled around and came to the cabin.

"Buckalew . . ."

Josh watched him distrustfully. "Yes?"

"Buckalew, I . . .." Quitman broke off, his face twisting. He held silent a moment, then said bitterly, "Aw, hell, what can a man say?" He turned and started after the wagon.

The first shot came from somewhere out in the fog, a long way off. Josh stiffened. He heard another shot, and a third, in quick succession.

Three guns. Even counting the old blunderbuss, Ramón had left here with only two. The fog seemed to close in on Josh. A hard chill paralyzed him. "Quitman, they're in trouble."

Quitman's face was grave. "Get your horse."

Aaron Provost wheeled the wagon around and brought his team back in a long trot. He shouted, "Daniel, give me your horse. You women and kids . . . back into the cabin!"

Josh told Muley to help Daniel guard the cabin. Quitman was out forty yards in the lead when Josh and Aaron and Jacob Phipps swung into their saddles. Josh spurred hard to catch up. Aaron and Phipps never did catch up, quite.

The cart's tracks were easy to follow, the wheels having pressed the curing grass deep into the soft, wet ground. Riding in a run, Josh listened for other shots. He heard none. Why hadn't there been more? The question ran again and again through his brain. Maybe they'd been overrun. He could think of several reasons, and he didn't like any of them.

Once he glimpsed Quitman's face and found it as fearful as his own.

Through the fog he saw the dark shape that must be the cart. "Yonder, Quitman, ahead of us."

They slowed their horses to a trot, wary, and only then did Aaron and Phipps catch up. Rifle cradled high, ready for trouble, Josh squinted, trying to see. The fog drifted a little, and he could make out the huddle of figures around the cart.

"There! They look like they're all right."

Ramón whirled, the rifle in his hands. He lowered it as recognition came. "Careful," he called. "They may still be around here."

Josh heard some of the children sobbing. He tried to see through the tight group of frightened figures. "Ramón, is everybody all right?"

The Mexican's face answered him before his voice did. "Josh, María is shot."

Josh hit the ground and dropped the reins. The children pulled aside to make room for him, but they stayed close to the cart, crouched in fear. María lay still.

"María!" Josh dropped to one knee. Miranda Hernandez gave him a quick glance, and he could see dread in her eyes. She had torn open the neck of María's dress and was pressing a crimson-soaked handkerchief to a wound above María's breast. Tears streaked Miranda's face. "It is bad, Josh."

Josh lifted the handkerchief. He gasped as he saw the ragged hole which a rifleball had torn. He put the handkerchief back in place. "Did it go all the way through?"

Miranda shook her head. "The ball is still in there."

"Then we got to get her to the cabin, and quick."

He looked up, and his gaze stopped at Ocie Quitman. The man's face was drained of color.

Aaron Provost was asking, "Ramón, where was they shootin' from?"

Ramón pointed toward the brush. In his nervousness he made no effort at English. "There. Two shots. I fired back one time. I heard two horses run away."

"Reckon they're all gone?"

"I have not tried to go and see."

Quitman's voice was cold. "*I'll* go see." He started walking.

Aaron shouted, "Quitman, if they're there, they'll kill you!"

Quitman did not slow down or look back. He kept walking, the rifle up and ready. He moved stiffly, as if whittled from wood.

María groaned. Voice breaking, Josh could only whisper. "You'll be all right, María, I promise. You'll be all right." He bent down and placed his cheek against her forehead, his eyes afire.

From out in the brush, Quitman called, "They're gone."

Cautiously Aaron and Jacob Phipps followed him. Josh looked up and saw Ramón through a blur. "Ramón, let's put her into the cart." They rolled out blankets to make as soft a bed as possible. It would be a rough ride back to the cabin, for there was no kind of spring or leather sling on these Mexican carts to take up any of the shock. By the time they had placed María on the blankets, the other three men were back.

Ocie Quitman looked gravely at the girl. "How is she?"

Josh shook his head. "Bad."

Quitman's chin dropped. His eyes were hidden by the brim of his hat. When he looked up again, his face was dark with a fury Josh had never seen. His voice was quiet and deadly. "It wasn't Indians. We found boot-heel marks out there, and tobacco juice."

Jacob Phipps said regretfully, "It was Dent Sessum and old Noonan."

Aaron said, "They must've thought we'd never look at their tracks. They been drinkin'; maybe they didn't think at all."

Ramón's eyes filled with tears. "They must have been after me. They hit María instead."

Josh held the girl's shock-cold hand. "We'll settle with them later. Let's get María back where we can take care of her."

Quitman reached out. "You got a pistol in your belt, Buckalew. I want it."

"What for?"

"I'm not waitin'. I'm goin' after them now. I can't go up against two men with just a rifle. Whichever one I shot, the other would get me while I reloaded."

"We'll all go, Quitman, together. But first we got to think of María."

"I *am* thinkin' of her, and I'm thinkin' of them that shot her. You stay with her, Buckalew. It's your place; she's your girl. She always was." Quitman reached and took the pistol out of Josh's belt.

Josh could see murder in his eyes. "We could be wrong. It could've been somebody else. It's the government's place to pass judgment."

"We're not wrong. And we got no government, not out here. I'll see you when I get back. You take good care of that girl, Buckalew."

Jacob Phipps blocked Quitman's path. "You figurin' on shootin' them wherever you find them?"

"Like a pair of killer wolves."

"I'll go with you, Quitman."

"Old Noonan's a friend of yours, ain't he, Phipps?"

"He used to be."

"Then you stay here. I don't want to fight *three* men." He shoved Phipps aside. Phipps called, "Wait, Quitman."

Quitman turned, eyes narrowed. "Don't you give me no trouble, Phipps." He stood a moment, his terrible eyes boring into Phipps until Phipps' chin dropped. Quitman swung onto his horse, rode out to the brush, paused a moment, then moved into the fog, following the tracks.

Phipps looked after him, frowning. "Old Noonan's a big talker and all, but he *has* been a fighter in his time. He'd fight again if Quitman was to corner him."

Josh said, "If we get the bullet out, and if we can tell María is goin' to do all right, we'll go help Quitman."

"That may not be soon enough. I think I'd best trail after him."

"You worried about him, or about Noonan?"

Phipps shrugged. "Both, I reckon. There was a time I thought a right smart of that old man, even with all his faults. I'd rather see him take his chances with a court than have Quitman shoot him down like a mad dog."

"There's no stoppin' Quitman right now. He's after blood."

"Maybe he'll cool off before he catches them. Anyway, I'll trail along."

Phipps rode off into the fog.

Josh rode in the cart, holding María's cold hand, feeling tears burn his eyes each time she moaned. Every little bit he would take up the handkerchief to let the blood wash the wound clean, then put it back again. Without help, she would have bled to death before now. Times, when he felt he was going to break down, Miranda would reach across and grip his arm. For a little woman, Ramón's wife had a lot of strength. "Faith, Josh. Faith."

They carried María into the cabin, the white-faced Rebecca Provost and Heather Winslow rushing ahead to clear a place for her. "The table," Josh said breathlessly. "We got to put her on the table and get the bullet out. You-all get some hot water started."

Aaron had planed down some boards riven from logs and had built Josh a heavy table, held together with stout pegs. Josh and Ramón placed María there on blankets

Heather had spread. Josh stood back, looking down on the still girl.

"We got to dig that bullet out. Who's goin' to do it?"

Everybody looked at somebody else. All eyes came back to Josh. He shook his head. "You women—you got skilled fingers."

Rebecca demurred. "It'll take a man to have the stomach for it."

Josh looked in vain to Ramón, for he could see Ramón beginning to weep. Aaron raised his own trembling hands. "A thing like this, Josh, I got ten thumbs. It's up to you."

María's eyes came partially open. She tried to speak, but the words were unclear. Josh leaned over anxiously. "Don't talk now, *querida*."

"Ocie . . ." she murmured. "Where is Ocie?"

Josh swallowed and looked away. Quietly he said, "He's around."

"I want him. I want him here."

A taste came to Josh's mouth, a taste like gall. But he whispered: "He'll be here, María. Don't you fret; he'll be here."

She lapsed back into unconsciousness. Cold sweat broke on Josh's face. "I don't know if I can do it."

"You operated on that bushwacker boy," Aaron said.

"And he died."

When the water was hot, he picked up a knife with a stiletto blade. He had to go by feel rather than sight because the blood kept welling up. Each time his hands started to tremble, he paused, taking a deep breath or two. And while he worked, he prayed. María stirred, the pain reaching her through her unconsciousness. Once Josh thought he would have to give up, for sickness rolled in his stomach. But from somewhere he took strength to keep on. And finally the ball came out. He dropped it, and it rolled against his boot on the dirt floor. He realized he'd held his breath a long, long time. He let out what had been compressed in his lungs and took a deep breath of fresh air. He let the wound bleed a moment to wash it clean, then called for a hot iron to sear it over. María lunged against him and cried out, then went limp.

Josh's tears flowed unchecked. "Jesus, don't let her die again!"

XIV

SITTING IN A ROUGH CHAIR BESIDE THE BED, HE HEARD a horse running. He raised his head to listen. He blinked the haze from his burning eyes and saw that Aaron and Ramón were listening too. Aaron went to the door.

"Can't see him for the fog. Way he's ridin', there's somethin' wrong."

There's a lot wrong, Josh thought numbly. *There's an awful lot wrong.* He pushed stiffly to his feet and dragged himself across the dirt floor to stand beside Aaron. Ramón had stepped into the yard. Jacob Phipps broke out of the fog, splashing across the creek and up the steep bank.

"Quitman's in trouble!" he shouted. "Indians!"

Josh heard, but he was too numb to move. It took a moment for the message to soak in on him.

Phipps shouted, "They got him cornered up in the limestone bluffs. I don't know how long he can hold out."

Aaron grabbed his rifle and went out the door. "How many?"

"Couldn't tell for the fog, not for sure. Seven or eight, maybe ten. Too many, that's for certain."

Ramón came for his rifle. He paused. "Josh, you coming?"

Josh looked at the girl. She hadn't moved or moaned or anything since he had seared the wound. Her face was almost gray. "María . . ." He clenched his fist. "We can't leave her now." Resentment came in an angry rush. "Dammit, he got himself into this. We tried to tell him."

"Maybe you should stay, then. We'll go to Quitman."

Josh touched the girl's hand and found it cold as ever. But there was still a pulse. "I don't want to leave her, Ramón. But she'd want me to go. Wait, and I'll get my rifle."

He rode hunched, his mind and soul still in that cabin and only the shell of him out here on horseback, riding in the fall chill. He only half heard Jacob Phipps telling what had happened.

"I trailed along behind him aways, and he must've caught on. All of a sudden he rode out from behind a live oak tree with his rifle on me and told me to get away and stay away, or he was liable to put a rifle ball through my other arm. I tell you, I was sore tempted to come on back. But I decided maybe I still ought to be around, so I let him have a long start, and I trailed him again. He come to the creek. The tracks led off down into the water. I reckon he figured the same as I did, that they was tryin' to throw off anybody that might come after them. But bein' who they was, they'd head in the general direction of Noonan's cabin. Quitman's tracks led thataway, so I followed.

"It was the fog that saved me when the Indians jumped him. They was so interested in him that they didn't see me. He must've had a little warnin', because I heard his horse runnin' before they ever started to whoopin'. He took out across the creek and headed west toward the bluffs, them Indians after him like hounds after a rabbit. There was too many of them for me to help him. I trailed along till I knowed he made the bluffs. I heard him fire a shot or two. After that, I turned and came back here." Phipps was apologetic. "I'd of stayed if there'd of been anything I could do. But they had him hemmed, and I couldn't have got through to him."

Aaron said, "You done the right thing."

Phipps turned to Josh. "How's the girl?"

Josh shook his head. "I don't know. I just don't know."

They came to the creek, and Josh could see the tracks where the Indians had gone up the opposite bank. Ramón pointed. "They were coming down the creek. Quitman was going up the creek, following Sessum and Noonan."

That brought Josh up with a shudder. "Then the Indians must've run into Sessum and Noonan before they found Quitman."

Phipps shivered. "I thought of that awhile ago. I figure Quitman wasted his trip. Them Indians likely already done to Sessum and Noonan what *he* was intendin' to do. *More,* even."

Josh managed to collect his wits. Perhaps what brought him to reality was the brutal certainty of what must have happened to that hapless pair of scoundrels. He wondered if it had been quick, or if the Indians had taken their time. When they weren't in any hurry, the Comanches had their ways. It wasn't a thing Josh would wish on anybody. But thinking of María, the cold clay color of her face when he had left her, he didn't care whether death had come quickly or not for Sessum and Noonan. He found no sympathy.

A vagrant thought ran through his mind: that hidden money wouldn't do Sessum any good now. Or anybody else, either. Chances were it would never be found.

Josh knew the bluffs Phipps had spoken of. He had sought wild cattle here many times, and mustangs. This ground was almost as familiar to him as his own yard and fields that he had plowed and harvested and built his cabin upon. "It's not far anymore," he said cautiously. "We better spread out a little and keep a careful watch. We don't want them jumpin' us by surprise. We'd rather have it the other way."

It worried him, the fact that by Phipps' account the Indians had them somewhat outnumbered. Josh had long heard people brag that a white man was the equal of several Indians in a fight, but he had taken that as idle boasting. The few hostile Indians he'd met hadn't been anything to mess around with. If Quitman was still alive, the best chance they had to rescue him was by using their one bit of leverage—surprise.

Somewhere ahead of them, he heard a shot. He saw some of the anxiety lift from Aaron's face. The farmer edged over to Josh. "Quitman's rifle. I know the sound of it. They ain't got him yet."

Josh eased a little. "He's likely found him a good place with the bluff to his back. They can't get to him except straight on."

Aaron nodded. "The Comanch, he loves a good fight, long as he knows he's goin' to win it. But he don't fancy suicide. They're probably just laid up there, figurin' on wearin' him down."

"Quitman's got his rifle and my pistol," Josh reasoned. "Long's he don't let both of them get empty at the same time, they'll show him a lot of respect. They know that sooner or later he's either got to come out or starve. Time don't mean much to an Indian."

Phipps said nervously, "Right now we need old Sam Houston to general for us. I don't like suicide any more than the Comanches do."

Josh found all the men looking to him for leadership. He didn't want it. He wasn't sure he knew enough to give it to them. He had no plan. All he'd thought of was that Quitman was trapped, and it was up to them to get him out of trouble. How, he didn't know.

Finally he said, "Since we know he's still there, let's go

easy; take our time and figure how we can do this right. Fog ought to let us get in pretty close."

They rode in silence, Josh watching for the outline of the bluffs to begin showing. Presently he heard another shot. Quitman's rifle. It occurred to him that the Indians probably had no guns, for he hadn't heard any. Only a scattered few rifles had fallen into Indian hands by trade, plus an occasional one stolen in a raid or taken from a murdered white man. Most Indians still didn't know how to load and fire a rifle even if they came into possession. But the bow could be as deadly as a rifle, within its range. Even more so, in one way, for a Comanche could unleash several arrows while a white man was reloading a rifle for just one more shot.

They were near the bluffs now. Josh knew, though he could not yet see them. He raised his hand for a halt. He leaned forward in the saddle, listening. He couldn't hear anything. He pushed on, slower now, watching where his horse stepped, keeping him away from rocks that he might kick and cause a noise. Josh's hand tightened on the stock of his rifle. He found himself breathing faster.

Then, from out in the fog, he heard the restless stamping of horses' hoofs. He held up his hand again and halted to listen. Somewhere up there, he reasoned, the Indians' horses were being held in a safe place away from fire. Josh swung down from the saddle and looked back. "Ramón," he whispered, "you want to go with me? Aaron, you and Jacob watch after our horses."

Ramón beside him, Josh walked carefully, watching his footing, peering cautiously through the fog. At length he saw something move, and he dropped to one knee, pointing. Ramón nodded.

There were the Indian horses. As the fog drifted, Josh glimpsed an Indian a-horseback, tending them. The brave's attention was not on the horses, however; he was looking westward, where the bluffs lay. After a few moments another rifle shot echoed against the unseen limestone walls, and the horses stirred restlessly.

Josh whispered, "He's not lookin' for any trouble from thisaway."

Ramón said, "You want to try to get him? I could use my knife."

Josh shook his head. "Not yet. If somethin' went wrong, he might raise an alarm before we're ready. Let's ease around him and see how the rest of them are spread out."

Crouching, they moved at a tangent from the Indian horses, carefully keeping to the live oak brush for cover, because now and again the fog drifted enough to leave them exposed for anyone who happened to be looking in their direction. In a little while the picture was clear to Josh. As he had expected, the warriors had spread themselves in a ragged line just back from Quitman's position at the base of the bluff. He was bottled up in there like whisky stoppered in a jug. Josh couldn't see him, though once he caught the flash of the rifle. He pointed, and Ramón nodded. He had seen too. Josh made a sign for retreat.

When they were back with Aaron and Phipps, Josh knelt and brushed away the mat of old live oak leaves and acorns so he could draw a rough map on the ground. "This here is the bluff. Right here is Quitman. The Comanches are scattered along like this . . . here, and here, and here. We couldn't see them all, but we took a count on their horses. There was ten, plus Quitman's." He glanced at Phipps. "Two of them horses belonged to Sessum and Noonan."

Phipps grimaced. "I figured that."

"If all the Indians was mounted to start with, and they picked up Sessum's and Noonan's horses extra, that comes out to eight men."

Aaron counted on his fingers. "Four of us. That's two to one."

"Quitman makes five. From where he's at, he can help."

Aaron frowned. "Never did go much for Indian-fightin', not even when the odds was in our favor."

"We got no choice, except to leave Quitman there. Likely these are braves out on a horse raid. If we don't stop them here they'll come on and hit one of us anyway . . . maybe all of us. We'll still have to fight."

Phipps asked, "You got a plan, Josh?"

Josh shrugged. "Not much. We just hit them and hope the surprise makes up for the difference in numbers."

Ramón said regretfully in Spanish, "Lately it seems all we've done is fight. The war, first. Then Mexican army stragglers, then that group of Redland renegades. Now the Indians."

Josh said, "It's a raw country. If we stay here there'll be more fightin' yet before we've won this land free and clear. And I intend to stay!"

Ramón replied, "If I fight now, perhaps my sons will never have to."

"Everybody has to fight, in his own way and in his own time. You're all ready to go, I hope."

They made a long arc to the left, walking their mounts slowly and watchfully. At length Josh put up his hand. "We've got them outflanked now. From here we can ride in on them and take them one at a time. The horses will be yonder." He pointed. "We'll rush the horses first and drive them right in on top of the Indians. If that don't confuse them, nothin' will."

He started to go on, but he hesitated. There was one more thing which needed to be said. His gaze moved from one man to another, and he spoke gravely. "Quitman's just one man. If he lives but one of us dies, we haven't gained anything. We've just swapped lives. I'm no hero and got no wish to ever be one. Let's just hit them hard and fast and make as little target as we can get by with."

They moved into a trot toward the horses. From up against the bluff, the rifle fired again. *Good,* thought Josh, *that'll hold their attention for a minute.* He leaned forward, straining to see the horses. When suddenly they showed through the fog, he saw that the Indian guarding them was still mounted, looking toward the cliff. Josh touched spurs to his horse and moved into a run.

Hearing him, the Indian turned, surprised. For a second or two he stared in disbelief. Then he brought up his bow with his left hand as his right hand reached back for an arrow from his quiver. Before the arrow touched the bowstring, Josh plowed into him. He drove the rifle butt into the warrior's ribs, then swung it up and jammed it against the chin. Grunting, the Indian slid over his horse's side, still clutching the bow, trying to bring the arrow to the string. Then Ramón was there, knife blade flashing. He leaned out of the saddle, the knife streaking down and coming up red.

The horses shied away, moving toward the Indians, Josh waved his hat and shouted. The other men started shouting, too. The horses broke into a run.

The first Indian jumped up from behind a scrub oak, consternation in his eyes. Not quite comprehending, he waved his arms and shouted, trying to turn the horses. They split around him. Josh's rifle butt slashed, and the Indian fell.

The racket stirred the others, who could not see clearly through the fog but knew instinctively that something had gone wrong. One by one the running horses sped past them or split around them. An arrow sang past Josh, and he saw an Indian whipping another arrow into place. Josh fired, knowing as he did so that for the rest of this run he was carrying an empty rifle. Well, by George, at least it would make a damn good club. He spurred and shouted and fell right in behind the running horses.

Another Indian arose, arrow fitted. Josh dropped down

over his horse's off-shoulder. He felt the impact as it struck his saddle, and a sudden burn told him it had at least creased his thigh. Another shot sounded behind him. The Indian fell.

Two shots gone. Only two shots left among us.

His horse stumbled, almost fell, caught its footing and ran again. But its movement was labored, and Josh saw the arrow driven into its shoulder.

I'll be lucky to finish this run before he falls.

In front of him, behind him, he could see the bewildered Indians, loosing arrows. The horse stumbled. Josh kicked free of the stirrups and hit the ground rolling, holding onto his rifle. He heard the rip of cloth and realized the arrow which grazed his thigh had pinned him to the saddle. He jumped to his feet, hopping, looking around desperately. He held the rifle in both hands, like a club.

Through the fog he had a clear view of the bluff now. He saw an Indian rise up and take aim at him, too far away for the clubbed rifle to help him. Partway up the bluff, fire flashed, and the Indian fell.

Then Phipps reined up beside him. "Up, Josh. Hurry!"

He offered Josh an empty stirrup, and Josh swung up behind him.

Ramón Hernandez spurred to the base of the cliff. Ocie Quitman clambored down to meet him. Ramón leaned over, extending his arm. Quitman caught it and swung up, landing on the horse's hips. An Indian came running to stop them. Ramón fired. The Indian dropped his bow and sank to his knees.

One shot left, Josh thought. *Wonder who has it?*

Aaron Provost slowed to wait for Ramón and Quitman. As a Comanche stepped from behind a live oak, Aaron squeezed off a shot. It missed, but it clipped leaves above the Comanche's head and showered them on him. His arrow went astray.

"Let's get out of here!" Josh shouted. Aaron came in a lope, waving his hat at the loose horses. Ramón and Quitman were just behind him. Looking back over his shoulder, Josh saw a couple of arrows in flight, but they would fall short.

We're out of their range.

They circled around the horses and brought them finally to a nervous, milling stop. Josh slid off, going to one knee and pushing back to his feet. He felt the thigh, and his hand came away with a small streak of blood. The arrow had not cut deep. "Anybody hit?" he asked anxiously.

No one else was except Ocie Quitman. Quitman's arm was bleeding. Stepping to the ground, Quitman slid up his sleeve and examined the wound. "Just enough to teach me humility," he said, "I'll live." His gaze lifted to Ramón, then went to Phipps and Aaron and Josh. "Men, I don't know what to say. I hope *thanks* will do."

Josh waited for someone to reply, but no one did. He said, "That's good enough. I expect you'd of done the same for any of us."

"They as good as had me. I was almost out of powder." He looked at Jacob Phipps. "You went and trailed me, even after I told you not to."

Phipps nodded. "Seemed like the thing to do."

Quitman turned to Ramón. "And you . . . you're the one who went in there and picked me up. You're the last one who had any reason to do it."

Ramón shrugged. "I had a reason. María."

A frown came over Ocie Quitman. He turned his face to Josh. "She's all right, isn't she? You wouldn't have left her if she wasn't all right, would you?"

Josh said tightly, "She looked bad when we left her."

"Then, you ought to've stayed."

"The women were there. They could do as much as I could."

Quitman stared at the ground. "Josh, I wonder why you came after me atall. I've caused you a right smart of trouble." He gripped his arm, where the stain was still spreading. "I think the best thing for me to do is take my son and go somewhere . . . to get away from here."

Josh said, "Let's talk about it later." He pointed to Quitman's horse, which stamped nervously among the Indian ponies, the saddle still on its back. "Right now you better catch that bay. I'll take Sessum's. I don't have the nerve to try to get my saddle . . . not right now."

Aaron gave him a boost up. Josh motioned. "Let's go see about María."

Rebecca Provost and Heather Winslow waited anxiously in the doorway as the men rode into view. Josh could see them counting fearfully, making sure no one was missing. Rebecca hurried out and threw her arms around Aaron as he stepped out of the saddle. Muley and the children came running, and Josh dropped his reins into the first pair of eager hands. Ocie Quitman grabbed up his son and gave him a fierce hug, then set him down. Together he and Josh walked to the door. Heather Winslow met them there. Tears stained her cheeks.

Josh asked with anxiety, "What about María?"

"She's conscious now. We tried to lie to her about where you'd all gone, but I think she knew."

Josh and Quitman stepped into the room and haltingly moved toward the bed where María lay. Her eyes opened, and she blinked, trying to recognize the men against the light of the open door. Her hand came up weakly, and she gave a sharp little cry. "Josh!"

"I'm right here, María."

"Did you find Ocie? Did you bring him?"

Josh halted. "We found him, María. He's here."

Quitman glanced at him in surprise. Josh gave him a nudge forward. "Go on. It's you she was callin' for when we took the bullet out. It's you she really wants, not me."

Quitman dropped his hat to the earthen floor and moved forward with slow, uncertain steps. He knelt beside the girl and said hoarsely, "I'm here. I'm here if you want me."

Her hand reached out, and he took it. "Yes, Ocie," she whispered. "I want you." He dropped himself down beside her, his cheek to her own. Josh could hear her sobbing quietly and thanking the saints.

Quitman was telling her, "I'm not a good man for you. You know me. I'm hard and I'm mean, and when I get an idea in my stubborn head, nobody can tell me I'm wrong."

"I am stubborn too."

"It won't be easy. You know how I've been. I'll be hard to change."

"But I want you, Ocie."

Throat tight, Josh turned and walked toward the door, where Heather waited. He tried to smile, but it was a poor attempt, and he gave it up. It hurt too much. "She'll live, Heather. She wants to, and she's a strong little woman, that María. Anything she wants bad enough, she'll get."

"And she wants Ocie Quitman."

Josh nodded.

Heather stared at him in wonder. "You'd give her up, just like that?"

Josh flinched. "What I'm givin' up is a dream, Heather, a mirage. María never was mine to give up, really. There was a time she thought she loved me, I guess, but she was just a girl. She hadn't met anybody else. I thought I loved her too, and in a way I did. I still do. But it was never right, not from the start."

He stepped outside and leaned against the wall, his gaze drifting aimlessly over the field, over the rolling prairie and the sun-cured grass. "She took me back, Heather; that's all it ever really was. When I was with María it was like she had come to me from somewhere out of the past, out of a time that was gone but that I never could quite turn loose of. She wasn't really María, not to me. She was always somebody else, somebody I had to say goodbye to years ago but never quite let go of. Deep inside me, I guess I've sensed it awhile now. That's why I never could bring myself to talk to her about marryin' me. While ago, when I took the bullet out, I found myself prayin' she wouldn't die again." His fist clenched. "Die *again*. It wasn't María I prayed for; it was her sister Teresa. It was *always* Teresa."

Heather waited a long time before she asked, "Do you think you can turn loose now?"

He nodded slowly. "It won't be easy, but I'll have to."

Heather took his hand. "Josh, I had to, once. Maybe, if you wanted me to, I could teach you how."

He turned and looked at her as if he had never seen her before. It occurred to him that he never really had. "Maybe you can, Heather. Maybe you can."